EXIT
WOUNDS

EXIT WOUNDS

Annie O'Neill Stein

THE PERMANENT PRESS
Sag Harbor, NY 11963

For information, address:
The Permanent Press
4170 Noyac Road
Sag Harbor, NY 11963
www.thepermanentpress.com

Library of Congress Cataloging-in-Publication Data

O'Neill Stein, Annie, author.
   Exit wounds / Annie O'Neill Stein.
   Sag Harbor, NY: The Permanent Press, [2022]
   ISBN: 978-1-57962-659-4 (hardcover)
   ISBN: 978-1-57962-660-0 (trade paperback)
   ISBN: 978-1-57962-661-7 (ebook)
      1. LCGFT: Bildungsromans. 2. Novels.

PS3615.N53 E95 2022 (print)   2022021728
PS3615.N53 (ebook)   2022021729
813'.6—dc23/eng/20220531

Printed in the United States of America

To All the Baby Ducks

I'm learning to live without you now.
But I miss you sometimes.
All the things I thought I knew, I'm learning again.
But I think it's about forgiveness . . .

—DON HENLEY, "The Heart of the Matter"

Prologue

IT'S THE NOT saying goodbye that can kill you. Not quickly, which could be merciful, but so slowly one doesn't even know it's happening.

Before a loved one dies, saying goodbye, making peace, speaking one's heart to the dying beloved, allows one to move forward. To be released and to release. For forgiveness to occur.

If that doesn't happen, one's heart could unknowingly be in a state of arrested development. In a word, fucked. One's heart could be fucked. Decisions will be made, diseases will be invited in, melancholy and moodiness will follow for the rest of one's days.

Such was the case with Laura.

CHAPTER 1

The Half-Assed Brother

"WHY DID THE man cut the toilet seat in half?" Laura's father asked when he'd stopped tickling her. She was laughing so hard she was almost crying. When the commercial for Rice Krispies, snap, crackle, and pop, interrupted *Howdy Doody* and Buffalo Bob, the human slob, her father had launched a sneak tickle attack. He stopped when he nearly fell off the bed, not because she begged him to.

"I dunno," she answered hiccuping, her white flannel pajamas with the pink jumping cows, her favorites, falling down. Yanking the bottoms back up while raking a wad of grown-out bangs back, she said again, "I dunno, Daddy, why?"

"Because his half-assed brother was coming to town," said her dad, delighted in himself, followed by a "Now there ya go," in his put-on Irish accent, picking her up, facing her toward the TV. Howdy was back saying, "Howdy, kids," so she turned her attention to the black-and-white television set on top of the mahogany trunk at the foot of her parents' bed, saving herself from showing him that she didn't get the joke. The trunk held extra linens, several wool blankets, and a stack of her mother's neatly folded satin bed jackets in a see-through plastic bag that leaked the scent of mothballs.

No one ever wanted to disturb the precious television set by going for another blanket on a cold night. As a family, they held the set in great esteem. Lassie was in there and Arthur Godfrey. For Laura and her dad, it was their boundary, their fourth wall, their chaperone. And an intricate part of their Saturday mornings.

When she turned her attention back to Howdy and Buffalo Bob, her dad took up his newspaper, the night before's *New York Herald Tribune*, or the *Wall Street Journal* from earlier in the week. He read while she watched. That was a sublime time, although she didn't know it then, as we never do, nor did she know the word to describe it.

Her mother may have been having her hair done in the village. For a while she had a standing eight thirty Saturday morning appointment with Sal, the owner of the only hair salon in their town. He was tall, handsome, charmingly Italian, her mom would tease him.

"Tell me again why you were banished to the Isle of Station Wagons? It's time we both went back to the land of crazy cabbies before the quiet out here buries us both," Sal would say.

Working the tail of his teasing comb through her hair, they'd be off comparing the things they missed back in the city. Schrafft's coffee ice cream for her. Any bakery in Little Italy for him.

If her parents were enjoying a good spell, a sober, healthy spell, her mother could have been downstairs making pancakes, scrambling eggs, and frying up perfectly crisp bacon. She may have been wrestling Aunt Jemima maple syrup out of Peggy's hands before she drank it all up like milk.

Peggy must have been around three then, as Laura was six when she and her father were in love.

He was long, lean, and prematurely gray, her dad. With thinning hair cut short at the sides and brushed back, just a little longer than his marine haircut; with blue eyes—ice blue—and sharp features. His mouth and eyes looked in cahoots, like they were always laughing. He was handsome, like the actor Lee Marvin (famous for playing marines in the fifties and sixties), only gentler looking, unless he was drunk past the line of pleasant, heading into cruel. But on Saturday mornings for a while there, none of that unattractiveness reared its ugly head. He was all hers for a couple of undisturbed hours, making Laura one heck of a happy daddy's girl.

Laura hadn't a clue where Lucy was on those Saturday mornings. She didn't care about either of her sisters' whereabouts during those sessions, if they weren't anywhere near her parents' bedroom.

"I'm gonna give you the business," her dad would say when she'd climb up on his chest and hold the neck of his undershirt. Feeling the cotton, warm and worn, between her chubby little fingers, she'd hoist it up to her nose and sniff it, inhaling her daddy.

"I'm giving you the business, young lady," he'd tell her again, diving full-on into her neck, making nuzzling sounds. An insect fiesta. A bee bumbling, a buzzing fly diving into her neck, while his hands spider danced over her back and belly. He may have been his truest, least-guarded self on those mornings. His freest, without the drink. No reason not to be free when all that's coming straight at you is love, pure love, wanting only to stick to you like a second skin.

Things must have been going well at home. Maybe he was selling a lot, going from door to door, smiling, tipping his hat for the Fuller Brush Company. Maybe it was later, after her Grandpa Curry bought him his seat on the New York Stock Exchange. He was feeling semi-buoyant about himself then, for sure. Whatever the reason, it was a healthier, happier, better period than those to come. The late fifties in suburban New York wasn't exactly a time of innocence and wonder that people wanted it to be. But they smiled in their plaid short-sleeved shirts, mowed their lawns, and tipped their hats to their neighbors.

When the Saturday morning snugglefests in her parents' bed ended, her father replaced them with Saturday afternoons at Rudy's bar. Grown-up stuff. Sporting his khaki trousers and a tweed jacket, he did what, culturally, came naturally to him. Irish men, by tradition, spent at least two hours of their Saturday afternoons in the "pub." Rudy's, the only freestanding watering hole in Sands Point, did a brisk business on Saturdays. All the "micks" came out of the woodwork thirsty. Firemen, policemen, and plumbers were your usual suspects. Lawyers, doctors, insurance brokers wearing sports jackets, a priest or two in a black cardigan, also constituted a typical Saturday afternoon with elbows pressed to the polished wood at Rudy's.

"Whaddya say, Mike O'Toole, and who might this young filly beside ya be?" Rudy asked jovially as they strolled through the door with the sun framing them briefly in a bright yellow haze.

"Howdy, Rudy me boy," responded Laura's dad, putting a hand on her shoulder, directing her toward the partially occupied row of maroon leather barstools. The stools they landed on that first trip became "their" stools. Picking her up, swinging her in the air around to the left, then around to the right, giving her a good whiff of his brown houndstooth sports jacket—wet wool, mothballs from the hall closet, and his Old Spice aftershave—he plopped her atop the stool. "This is my partner in crime, Rudy," he said, "my middle girl, my little Laura."

That became her handle at Rudy's. She'd walk in the door and get greeted by the proprietor first, and then the regulars as "Little Laura." Oh, and how she loved it. How grown-up it made her feel, to strut her blue-jeaned self, with her bobbed haircut and white Keds, strut into that smoke-clouded, semi-dark den and be called by her very own nickname. Have her Shirley Temple waiting by a bowl of peanuts in front of her "regular" place at the bar. Rudy and the others didn't know Lucy and how pretty she was, or Peggy, with her button nose and cute lisp. No, her new friends didn't even know they existed, which was fine with her. Laura with her round face, just a backdrop for a million freckles, felt she couldn't compete with either "pretty" or "cute." So a nickname in a bar was a gift.

Laura felt guilty about playing both sides of the fence for a while. She and her dad were supposed to be doing errands on Saturdays. The dry cleaners to pick up his suits, grocery shopping at the A&P, the library to pick up a book for her mother. On their way out the door, her mother always asked her to "be a good girl now, and keep an eye on your father." No fool, Margaret O'Toole.

Her mother thought Laura was her sole sidekick and relied on her more than her other two daughters. But her mother was completely in the dark about her activities with her dad. She would assure her mother, she would, keeping her eyes to the ground.

She didn't think of it as lying. Omitting was what it was, but she saw it as leaving that part out. Her mother's question when they got home was always, "Was your father good?" or "Did your father behave himself?" She always told the truth because he was indeed good to her, and everyone else at Rudy's, where he behaved very well. He was funny and made her laugh. Made several of the men laugh, including Mr. O'Hara, Sean O'Hara, the father of the fat boy in her class, and Sergeant Sullivan, whose wife waved the school kids across the street at the light in front of George's luncheonette. Her dad had them all in stitches.

"Ah, go on, Mike, you're a real card, you are," said Mr. O'Hara.

"He is indeed," agreed Rudy, drying a glass with a rag behind the bar, the burly white-haired caricature of an Irish barkeep, shaking off the last of his laugh. "Little Laura," he'd say, turning to her, "can I top off your Shirley fer ya? Another cherry perhaps? Your old man's a real pistol, missy!"

Her father was a card and a pistol at Rudy's, so she determined that qualified as well behaved. The only reason she didn't feel too guilty about straddling both sides of the fence was that she told herself it would be handing her parents another reason to ruckus. Their list was long enough. At six she was no fool either.

Behind the bar at Rudy's, parked in front of the mirror that lined the wall from floor to ceiling, sat a beautiful model ship. It was handmade of a dark wood and every intricate piece of it was delicate, beautiful, and fascinating to Laura, who had never seen one like it. After a few Saturdays asking Rudy about the ship, he began to take it down and put it near her place alongside her Shirley. She'd see him taking it from behind the bar when he saw them coming in. Rudy took excellent care of that boat. It never had a speck of dust on it. He loved all kinds of boats and could rattle off the names of famous seafaring vessels from all over the world 'til you'd drop your head in the crook of your arm flat down on the bar. Snoring from boring was how the regulars joked about it. Some of the men ribbed him, saying things to Rudy like, "Ya buying her for your retirement, Captain." But she and Rudy shared an affinity for that model ship. Laura could sit for hours studying every detail of it. Rudy told her that he built it in 646 consecutive days. He said it was a long time ago, when he needed a project to come home to 646 days in a row. That he was a different man when he finished from who he was when he started. "See how I customized the porthole?" Rudy pointed that out to her one Saturday afternoon while her father was holding forth on the merits of owning a Mercury. Especially the station wagons. She was in their clubhouse. Ships. Cars. Half-assed brothers coming to town.

The outings to Rudy's lasted several months. Being the only child on those afternoons didn't bother her a bit. She knew she didn't belong there, just as she knew it wasn't appropriate for her to be running into the Sands Point Liquor Locker to get her mother a fifth of Beefeater gin on the way home from school, but so far neither "outing" had harmed anyone. Again, it was her special time with her dad. She loved the way he looked in his sports coat and smelled of aftershave and was a "real card." She could tell he was proud of her in front of Rudy and his bar friends. She couldn't imagine him sharing Rudy's with either of her two sisters. He never had to ask her not to discuss their outings with either of them. She was born a savvy accomplice. He never got out of line there. He had a drink or two and nursed those for as long as he could. For as much time as he could steal. Laura's time at Rudy's laid the foundation for her lifelong proclivity toward illicit acts and clandestine hideaways.

Who knows how long they could've had at Rudy's? If cartoons in bed turned into cocktails at two, late suppers could've been close at hand had her father not fucked it up. The last time they went there as a couple, when she wasn't sent in to fetch him by her fuming mother waiting out in the car, was the day after she saw him give her mother a black eye. They didn't walk in as the happy couple or the giggling partners in crime that Saturday. The only reason she was even with him was because of the A&P errand front. She told her mother earlier that morning that she hated her father and wanted nothing to do with him, that if she were smart, she'd divorce him. But her mother insisted she go and help with the marketing. She was also told to "keep both eyes on him."

Her mother wore black sunglasses to hide the jellyfish-shaped bruise that bled purple down her left cheek past the rim of her glasses. Laura followed the shades of purples as her mom spoke. The night before, she had begged and pleaded that he unclench his fist and not punch her mother.

Things had gone badly from the get-go that night. She and Lucy were playing seven-card rummy in the back seat of the car parked in the train station lot waiting for the 5:25 from Penn Station to pull in. Elvis was singing "Don't be Cruel" on the radio. It was autumn and already dark and chilly. They hadn't changed out of their school uniforms and just had light sweaters over their jumpers. Their mom was smoking so her window was down, letting in the cool evening air and the fall smells Laura loved. Wood burning from neighboring fireplaces, wool sweaters, leaves going from pungent green to decaying red. The smell of grilling meat and roasting garlic from Peter's Grill across from the station made her hungry.

"I won!" Laura said, putting her cards down on the mid-section of the seat. "Shit, he's staggering," said her mother from up front. She and her sisters, all ears and eyes then, their game, history, searched the suited-up commuters to see how pronounced a stagger her mother was talking about.

"Well, girls," she continued, one hand holding her lit cigarette, the other slapping the back of the seat beside her, turning to them, "he's plastered tonight all right," giving her kids a look that said, "We're in for it, girls." And they were.

Sometime around midnight, wearing her PJs and tears of exhaustion, Laura leaned against a wall in her parents' bedroom. Weary and wrung out from hours of refereeing, detouring, and deflecting nasty, hurtful words and sentences spit from one parent's mouth to the other's, she pleaded, "Daddy, please, you love Mommy and Mommy loves you, please. Daddy, go to bed, you both need rest." Begging, crying, she put her body in between theirs when they got too close.

"You go to bed. This isn't your business, young lady. Get to bed," said her father, wearing nothing but his boxers. Skinny legs and all. Wobbling around, working to maintain footing.

"Leave her alone, Mike," slurred her mother, not quite as drunk as he was, wiping spit from her mouth with the back of her hand. Her hair and eyes vied for first place as to which looked wilder. "Leave us both alone, you bastard," she said. Before the words were even fully slurred out, he hit her. Laura never saw it coming. The punch hit her mother in the left eye and cheekbone, flung her into the wall, sending them all reeling.

She sat at her place at the bar, mute, not touching her Shirley Temple. She had a paper napkin in her hand and kept rubbing the bow of the ship with it. Silently, gently going over it, and over it, and over it again, speaking not a word to anyone. Rudy noticed the palpable silence and icicle air between her and her father. He asked, his eyes clearer and kinder than she remembered noticing before, if she was okay.

"Doin' all right there? Yer looking a might sad today," said Rudy, his protruding girth, wrapped tightly in an immaculate white apron, heaving out a sigh as he said it. Manly like. A big-bellied blacksmith, or a grandfatherly shoemaker from the old country. Or an Irish barkeep who'd pretty much seen it all.

"I'm okay, Rudy," she said unconvincingly, tracing the smooth wood. "I won't be coming back here so I'm saying goodbye to the ship." Her heart was broken. She loved her father, but then hated him is what she could've said, and he would've believed her.

"I see," was all Rudy said. She sat waiting for her father to down his drink with not a comment to share with anyone. Feeling sad to be giving up the ship, and Rudy's, she wanted to hate them both as much as she hated her father. When he finished his drink, he dug into his pocket, pulled out some bills and, standing, threw them on the bar.

"See ya, Rudy," he called back, heading toward the door, not even checking to see if his daughter was following him.

"Catch ya later, Mike," said Rudy. "Little Laura," he called out before she reached the door. "Come 'ere, miss," he said, and when she walked back to him, he picked up the ship and walked it around the bar to her.

"Take it, kid," he said. When she started to protest, he pushed the boat into her arms, turned her toward the door whispering so no one else could hear, "Take it, me darling, she's a sturdy one. Just like you."

CHAPTER 2

Bless Me, Father

IT WAS PAST midnight, like it usually was when the "fuck yous" and "no good bastard" started. The violence of their words and of their blows was nothing new. Laura's parents fought nightly or almost nightly for a good two-year stretch. Mostly verbal, the occasional physical jousting left her mother with black eyes, swollen purple, fading to yellow with time, and red welted arms. Her mother wore her marks silently with whatever guilt, shame, and dignity she possessed. But she was never passive.

That night it was different. Laura was there. She would've preferred to be fast asleep, like a normal third grader, resting up for the next morning's spelling test, but that wasn't an option. There she was, standing in the doorway of her parents' bedroom, yet again. Laura could see that her mother was in no shape to do the dance that night. Her eyes looked like they needed quiet, safety. Like she wanted to sleep it off. She wanted morning. Her face was sad, not fierce, and her voice not instigating, the way it was on other nights. Laura heard a tiredness in her soul for the first time and it broke her heart.

The strap of her mother's pink nightgown had fallen off her left shoulder. The fabric of the gown was transparent, so Laura saw all there was to see. The narrow white folds of flesh, her pubic region, and the raw red rope of a scar above it, from where the doctors had removed her three daughters. Her right breast drooped a bit lower than her left. Her arms and legs looked like white stick figures drawn by a child. At that moment her mother looked like a child. A lost, torn, and tattered child unable to enunciate her own daughter's name.

"Lau," there was no volume in her whispered word. "Go back to bed, sweetie. It's okay," she slurred, pulling her nightgown strap up her right hand, fingers fanned out, holding on to her shoulder bone like it was a branch. An exterior part of herself that might steady her. She tried to accompany her words with a small pathetic smile.

Laura left the room. Camping out in the hallway, crouching down a few feet away from her parents' door, she prayed. "Please God, I'll be the best girl ever, you'll see. I'll give all my allowance to the pagan babies starving in Africa, I'll stop saying how much I hate Lucy, and pay attention in church on Sundays. *Please*," she prayed, feeling selfish, "just make them stop so I can go back to sleep." The prayer was nothing but a habitual response. A way of coping with fear and fatigue. God wasn't listening.

Laura knew that. She'd been to see her parish priest, Father Donovan, several weeks before that particular ordinary night. She didn't know who else to go to and was under the misguided impression that the priest could talk to God for her. One night after dinner she walked the four blocks from her house, walked past the elementary school, the church, and up the wide red brick stairs to the rectory door. She rang the bronze bell to the left of an uninviting black door, shaking like a leaf, knowing she had to tell someone what was going on in her house. Someone holy and close to God. Someone who could help before it was too late. Someone who could keep a secret and sanctify her tattletales.

It was her mother she needed to protect. She didn't give a shit about ratting out her father.

"Bless me, Father, but they're drinking like fish and slapping each other around, and I'm scared someone might not wake up one morning," was her testimony. "Please, Father Donovan," she begged, "it's a nightly battle and I can't do my homework and I can't sleep, and they swear . . ." And they say "shit" and "fuck" and I can't see my father hit my mother one more time without wanting to kill him myself. She said that last part to herself. She couldn't bring herself to say "shit" and "fuck" in front of the priest.

She sat there spilling her guts to that man of God, graying and overfed, his blue eyes runny, his nose sporting those red spidery veins. God's representative here on Earth, the closest she figured she could get to Jesus Christ, the Savior, was sitting there smugly with tell-tale signs of being a drunk himself.

"They drink every night, Father. My dad comes home from work already half drunk. He starts drinking at the office, my mother says, then has a few on the train and, by the time the 5:25 from New York City pulls into the station, you can practically smell him before you see him.

"You're half drunk," her mother would say, leaning over to open the front passenger-side door of our station wagon.

"Well, you look like you've started cocktail hour on your own," he'd shoot back, slamming the door hard. My sisters and I, we just looked at each other as if to say, "Here we go again."

"Please, Father," she repeated several times to the priest, shaking, the adrenaline pumping as if she were walking home after dark when the wind picks up and rattles the trees. Getting scareder and scareder the darker it got.

There was something about the room they were sitting in. The "small parlor room," the priest's housekeeper called it, by the front door. Every time she heard a sound,

someone walking out on the street, a floorboard creaking
as the housekeeper walked by, she was afraid someone
would come in. Should she shut up and run out? Dark and
cramped with too much furniture and enough lace doilies
to curtain a whole house, the room's tobacco and camphor
smell brought on a wave of nausea.

She stared at the dark mustard-colored walls, which
were littered with pictures of Jesus as a child, one with baby
lambs out in a field, others with him sitting beside Joseph,
his father, in a sawdust-covered carpenter's studio or on his
mother's knee. Mary and Joseph, looking happy and sober
in every shot, gave Laura the courage to go on.

"My mother isn't well," she said, defending her mother
as she always did, her job for as long as she could remember. "She's lost babies and has had tumors removed. She
only drinks because she's in pain," Laura said to Jesus's
representative.

He looked like he could use a drink himself right about
then. He cleared his throat and began to fidget with his
collar. He pulled the clean end of his handkerchief out of
his pocket, wiped his brow, and Laura sensed her time was
limited with that guy, so she rushed on.

"He's going to kill her one day," she said, pumping it up
to get the priest's attention.

"He's the one that needs to be dealt with." She tried to
stress that to him.

"Even though my mother drinks nightly and during the
day before we get home from school," she admitted. Assuring him, with every vein that felt like it was bulging out of
her neck, though, that it was her father who was the problem. Her mother was sick. Her mother was in pain. Her
mother, drinking aside, was a saint. Her father, though, was
a criminal.

Laura was overcome with a pent-up need to have the
insanity stop. Just stop and be replaced by the kind of life

Ozzie and Harriet and their sons, David and Ricky, had. Or that slightly dumb, but oh-so-normal June Cleaver. She sure ran a happy household. That gang was the epitome of mid-fifties domestic bliss.

Laura knew at that point, as sure as she knew that if she spit on his outfit, the priest would slap her and call her the devil, that that guy was really itching for a drink. That telling him anything was just wasting her time. When he took her hand in his own moist, fleshy, trembling hand and led her to the front door, that was confirmed.

"Laura, now you go home and say five Our Fathers, five Hail Marys, and invite the baby Jesus into your heart." Walking her to the door, he left out "and I'll go get a martini."

Later she had almost fallen asleep crouched down with her back held up by the hallway wall outside of her parents' room, looking like one of those Chinese people she'd seen in her geography book, wearing pajamas, squatting against old, faded doorways. Where was that Baby Jesus now, she wondered. The next set of swearing had her upright. Her parents were on the move, bare feet slapping cold floor, and headed for the hallway.

"Come 'ere you," her father slurred at her mother. "You, that big shot father of yours, and all his money." Starting with the old refrain again, railing against his father-in-law for being wealthy "lace-curtain Irish" while his family was "straight off the boat," he pulled her mother out of their bedroom and into the hallway.

Yanking her hands out of his, trying to swing at him, but swiping only air, her mother cried out a deflated, "Bastard."

With a clump of gray hair covering one eye, the other exposed, looking mean and frozen on his wife, he took a step or two toward the stairs. He then grabbed a handful of her mother's hair from the top of her head, dragging her toward the stairway. With dark brown strands spilling out from in between his fingers and a ferocious look on his face, he dragged her mother down the stairs.

She let out a cry. One flight, across a wide landing, then down another flight, head smacking, bones cracking audibly. Nightgown shimmying up, exposing white legs, loose flesh. Exposing her womanhood to her children, who were, all three, at that point, up and out of their beds, lining the upstairs hallway in their pink Dr. Denton's with feet. Screaming in unison. Whatever violence Laura had seen couldn't hold a candle to that. She ran down the stairs, fists beating him and legs kicking.

Her mother's eyes bulged, her throat gasped for air, lips moving like those of a fish desperately caught on a hook. Shocked, fighting for life; caught off guard.

Her father's half-demented Irish mother, an unwelcome houseguest for well over a year by then, dressed in her black night clothes, was out in the hallway picking Peggy up in one arm, waving a crucifix with the other. Shouting like she was back on the streets of County Cork, the old lady cried, "Stop! Son, stop! Michael O'Toole, I'm tellin' ya now, stop!" She worked that crucifix as if the little silver Jesus would jump off and save the day, or at least Laura's mother.

Her older sister, Lucy, who usually stayed curled up under her bed like a dust ball during the fights, put both hands over her ears (futile, like Laura's prayers) and ran down the back stairs to hide behind the door separating the kitchen from the pantry. Laura yelled to her, "Call the police, dial the operator, tell them to send the police!"

Grabbing the back of her father's undershirt, Laura screamed again, "Get the police!"

The station house was about five minutes away from their house. Despite knowing that nine out of ten, whoever showed up would be an Irishman and one of her father's drinking buddies from Rudy's, she had no other choice.

When he'd dragged her all the way down to the first-floor landing, he let her go. Her father reeled, as if the impact of her landing had stunned him back into his own body. Pushing him out of her way, Laura dropped to her knees beside her mother when she heard the pounding on the front door. The policeman, shouting his arrival, sure enough, called her father by name. "Mike, what's going on here?" Laura was still kneeling over her mother, checking for breath, and pulling her nightgown down at the sound of the knocking. In the surreal midnight timing, where things seem to happen simultaneously while moving in slow motion, her father answered, "My wife had a fall." Lucy, freeing herself from behind the kitchen door, suddenly ran forward with "My mom fell down the stairs!" The pain and urgency in her sister's voice were from wanting that to be the case so badly it hurt.

Picking her hand up from the small of her mother's back, Laura opened her mouth and was about to scream, "No, he's killed her! Handcuff him, take him away, lock him up," when she was stopped by the faint whisper coming from the floor.

"I fell," was all her mother said. Laura heard her. Even whispered, her mother was telling her, in no uncertain terms, that was the only way to go.

After her father and the officer carried her mother to the living room couch, her father promised to call the doctor and the officer exited the way he entered. His voice registered polite concern, a slight embarrassment, like it was Christmas day and he'd stayed for an extra eggnog and was pretending to be needed back at the station. Then, in a voice that wasn't hers but came from deep within her, Laura commanded her father to go back upstairs to bed. As if grateful to be taking orders from an eight-year-old, staggering up the stairs in his baggy urine-stained Brooks Brothers boxers, he did just that. Lucy, pale, but also looking grateful, shot up the back stairs to the warmth and temporary safety of her bed.

Gathering up the lap blanket from her mother's blue armchair, Laura gently laid it across her mother's body, and then lay down beside her. She was afraid of moving in too close, afraid of holding her the way she wanted to, afraid of curling her body around her mother's and holding her tight. Her mother, the wounded sparrow. Stroking her hair, whispering softly, "It's going to be okay, Mommy, it's going to be okay." Laura prayed that was true until they both fell asleep.

CHAPTER 3

Driving to Quogue

It WAS THE summers Laura spent at her grandfather's house in Quogue that enabled her to survive her childhood. In her grandfather's day, people who summered in Quogue, a demure village sandwiched between Westhampton and Southampton near the end of Long Island, weren't the sort to use expressions like "The Hamptons." They simply called it "the country" or "the beach."

Her older sister, Lucy, who remembered little, yet marveled at, as well as loathed, Laura's ability to recall the details of their childhood, always, when speaking of their youth, brought up the one memory she allowed herself to vocalize, the driving to Quogue incident.

The entrance to her grandfather's property was marked by two massive stone columns, each bearing a discrete plaque engraved with the words "Sea Shadow." Up a long stretch of winding road, after tires had ground and spit more than their fair share of gravel, one would be greeted by green splendor. With horses on the left, and a family of sheep in full white coats grazing on the lawn to their right, they would approach the sprawling, brown-shingled main house at the center of the property. An army of roses, rows deep on both sides, guarded the expansive front porch. That setting, the graveled driveway a half a mile long, the animals, the roses, the house that sat so proudly and loomed so large, made Laura's heart stop and, young as she was, gave her a sense of worthiness. Even as a child, she knew the setting was miles above what her father's mother, dressed in black and waving her crucifix, had come from.

Normally a three-hour car ride from their house to Sea Shadow, the drive on the day both Lucy and Laura remembered stretched into an all-day affair due to their mother's incredibly drunken driving.

At each pit stop, her mother refueled herself, sipping from the little silver flask tucked into her smart, white, summer handbag. "Hand me my bag, girls," she would say to all her three daughters in the back seat, knowing one would respond.

It was fun for a while, Laura and her two sisters in identical madras Bermuda shorts, and identical Buster Brown— "The Boy in the Shoe"—haircuts singing along with the radio, bare legs sweating out puddles that squished as they squirmed back and forth on the red leatherette back seat. Their mother, in her pearl-studded cat-eye sunglasses, silk scarf holding back her brown hair, moved her red lips, mouthing the words to the songs. She looked too glamorous to be a drunk, though her mouth, which drooped a bit at the corners, and continued to droop throughout the drive, was a dead giveaway.

The ride accelerated from fun into that familiar stomach-fluttering, nail-biting display of nervousness three-quarters into it, when the car began to figure skate from lane to lane. Laura's mother cha-cha-cha-ing from accelerator to brake, was driving, once again, to the sound of her own drummer. At that point Laura wished her father was driving and not taking the train after work. He, for all his faults, was a better drunk driver.

"Get off of me," yelled Peggy, who'd been trying to lose herself in styling her Betsy Wetsy's hair when Laura landed in her lap abruptly. "Sorry," Laura mumbled, lifting herself off her sister's lap and Betsy's pink plastic belly. When their mother slammed down on the brakes for some reason other than need, Laura flew, freckled face first.

The girls had stopped singing "I found my thrill on Blueberry Hill," ("thrill" sung as "Phil" due to the large amount of missing front teeth from the mouths of the young trio), while Peggy started snarling, "My Betsy's gonna peepee all over you."

"Your doll's stupid and so are you!" Lucy said.

"I'm going to kill you both, pee on all your dolls, and cut their hair." That last threat was from Peggy again, the youngest and quietest of the sisters, who, in her own semi-silent way, was always violently mutilating her older sisters' dolls.

Their mother changed her tune as well. "Shut the hell up," she screamed, not sang, from up front where she was looking less glamorous by the second. Lipstick smeared, the pearl-studded sunglasses lopsided, and the telltale twitch at the corners of her mouth had begun working overtime. The breeze from the open windows couldn't defuse the smell of cigarette smoke, gin, and fear that permeated the car.

There was a large duck farm right before Westhampton with an enormous white-and-yellow plastic duck out front. Peggy loved the initial big duck sighting. It must have stood thirty feet tall and looked so lifelike in its plastic glory. The duck farm was a veritable festival of ducks. Running ducks, sitting ducks, scattering, squawking, and quacking ducks. Ducks over every inch of the damn place. When their mother swerved to the right and ran up on the curb and onto the farm's front lawn doing sixty miles per hour, those ducks ran for their little yellow lives! Wings flapping, feathers flying, chaos and high commotion.

Peggy, five at the time, started screaming, "Mommy's killing the ducks, Mommy's killing the ducks!" Lisping that full-tilt boogie, as their mother scattered the squawkers in all four directions. She didn't kill any ducks, not a one, as far as they could tell, but that was only through the grace of God.

Arriving at Sea Shadow, Paula, the housekeeper, who had been alerted by the gardeners having witnessed the car swipe one of the columns and careen up the driveway, muffler scraping gravel, was there, arms folded over her ample black bosom, to greet them. Paula, with her gray hair piled up on the top of her head like a bird's nest made of old Brillo pads, all crusty and coppery around the edges, talked Laura's mother gently out of the car. Walking up the front-porch stairs, she kept up a running monologue and kept a firm grip on her elbow.

"Miz Margaret, you had yourself some exciting ride, in such a hurry to get home! Uh-huh, you need you a nice nap. That's right, honey, you hold on to that banister. The senator's out fishin' with your brothers. You know he likes to see his favorite chil' looking well rested. Just a few more steps . . ."

While Paula verbally guided, Tiny, the cook—having been pulled out of her kitchen by Paula on her way out to the rescue—took care of Laura and her sisters.

Tiny smelled like chocolate chip cookies no matter what she was cooking. She was the complete opposite of her name. Every summer one of Laura's smart-mouthed cousins would ask her why she hadn't been named Biggie instead of Tiny. Her answer would always be the same.

"I 'spect if they'd known how big I'd grow to be, they would've. Come on, give big Tiny some sugar!" The inquisitive child would then be lost in the world of Tiny's chocolate-colored flesh.

"Who wants cookies fresh out my oven and to walk down to the barn 'n' see them new kittens?" Not waiting for the "I do I dos," she ushered the girls toward the barn, pulling cookies out of her apron pockets like bunnies out of a hat. The almost dead ducks and their fiesta of flying feathers history.

That was Lucy's memory. Her heirloom memory, the one not plastered over with decaying, yet endless to-do lists, school calendars, her children's gold-starred accomplishments, and dentist appointments. That memory hung sadly, limply, in a single strip where Lucy could grab it as needed. It's the one that started her sister's tongue clucking in genuine bewilderment as to how their mother could've driven them from one end of Long Island to the other, dead drunk. Laura used to waste time wondering about that herself.

Then she grew up. Got a whole life going that she worked her ass off to keep afloat. Then one day she saw it. Flashing like a neon marquee. Who among us couldn't use a little help getting home?

After all, as she said to Lucy when her sister started in with the tongue clucking, at the end of the day, all the little ducks lived.

CHAPTER 4

Holiday Haven

CHRISTMAS AT HER grandfather's Park Avenue apartment ran a close second to summers in Quogue. Whatever went on at Laura's house was forgotten the moment she stepped into the mammoth foyer of her grandfather's building. Walking into the life she could've or should've had, had her mother not married beneath her.

The world her mother and her nine siblings were raised in was a world furnished in Louis XIV and covered in French silk. A world where they were driven by chauffeurs, and had their meals prepared by cooks, served at a properly set table on fine English china. Laura knew her father hailed from the world of corned beef and cabbage.

In her house, most of the china was chipped or broken from being thrown at one parent by the other. The house was a fixer-upper no one ever got around to fixing up. The sofas in the living room and the chairs in the dining room were covered in the same blue French silk her grandmother's decorator had used in the Park Avenue apartment. It had been a gift, along with several good oriental rugs, to her parents when they bought the house. The good oriental rugs, worn, torn, and stained, were riddled with moth holes and patterned with dog pee.

The holidays—Thanksgiving, Christmas, and Easter Sunday—were celebrated at her grandfather's apartment until his death in 1962. Laura had referred to both the summer house in Quogue and the apartment in New York as being her grandfather's because that's the way she thought of them, her maternal grandmother having died when Laura was four. She never had a sense of her grandmother in either of the two homes. And the one memory she did have of her, a diminutive woman who bore ten children, she may have dreamt up. Her grandmother was in a hospital bed: short, rotund, with the family's blue eyes, wearing a white satin bed jacket. She was holding out a clear glass jar of Schrafft's sour balls, yellow, orange, and lime, perfect and glistening, offering Laura one. Her grandfather, whom everyone but his children and grandchildren referred to as "The Senator" out of respect for the two terms he served in the New York State Senate, like his wife, was diminutive in size. He had a large personage that announced his arrival and left his mark. He was also a damn dapper dresser. When Laura saw him in her mind, he was always in a pinstripe suit with a gold pocket watch attached to the vest. The navy-blue suit worked well with his white hair and frameless spectacles. His shirts were perfectly starched and white, and the ties so simple as to be unmemorable. She was partial to the memory she held of him watering his roses in front of the house in Quogue. A solitary round figure in navy blue shorts that showcased his bulbous vein-lined calves, a creaseless white linen summer shirt, and his Panama hat, he was the lord of the manor. It was his meditation, to water his roses. When Laura was a little girl, she loved arriving in Quogue early on a summer Friday, unpredictable as the drive might be, and catching sight of her grandfather, green garden hose in hand. Dignified, yet of the land. She was always caught between being both proud and in awe of him. Whenever in his company, she couldn't take her eyes off him.

Thanksgivings and Easter Sundays her aunts and uncles could spend with in-laws, if they had to, but Christmas was the day all her grandfather's ten children, their spouses and offspring spent together at 1120 Park Avenue. Her parents and aunts and uncles called it "1120," the way people called her grandfather "The Senator."

"See you at 1120," or, "There's a cocktail party at 1120," Laura would overhear her mother say into the phone. "Daddy's coming home from Europe today and going straight to 1120." Laura would overhear her and know she was talking to one of her four sisters. They were a large lot, five boys and five girls, her mother being the eldest. When Laura got older, she used to think of her grandmother, dead at the age of fifty-three from breast cancer, and about how she spent most of her adult life either pregnant, birthing, or nursing babies. She wondered to herself if all those hungry little sucklings at her breasts caused the cancer.

Christmas morning at her house was always fine. No matter how much drinking had been going on, how sick her mother was, or how broke her father was feeling, her parents both believed in Christmas. Laura thought they saw it as a time to make up to their three little girls. To say, "We're sorry we drink like fish, fight like cats and dogs, and live like pigs. Here, have a Patti Playpal doll." God bless them, they always put up a tree, had wrapped presents under it, and made sure each of their girls got a few of the things they had asked for. One Christmas Eve, Laura even caught her father down in the basement putting training wheels onto a new tricycle for her sister Peggy.

Christmas morning the girls would wake at the crack of dawn, tiptoe down to the dining room where the tree was, and rip open the presents, just like the kids on TV. They would play happily, yet quietly (so their parents got plenty of sleep), for hours. Then their mother would come downstairs in her pink satin robe, looking a little worse for wear, and start the bacon and eggs. Laura's mother's culinary specialty was scrambled eggs. She cooked them slowly, stirring constantly so they weren't lumpy but fine and wet, then gave them a sprinkling of paprika right before serving them. Her father would come down either in his boxers and undershirt (bad night) or his plaid bathrobe (better night), and the girls would show off what Santa brought. She and her sisters would give their parents the badly wrapped, handmade or drugstore-bought gifts they had for them. Perfume by Coty, Old Spice, picture frames made from old Popsicle sticks, which their parents would pretend to like. Then they'd sit down to those scrambled eggs and sausages like they were Donna Reed and the gang.

After breakfast, Laura and her sisters played under the tree a bit longer, then they all got ready for the eleven o'clock late Mass. An hour would have elapsed since breakfast, the official waiting time between food and the wafer, so her parents would both be able to take communion like sinless Catholics. They would swallow the body of Christ, with not spotless but perhaps contrite hearts, praying to do better. She and her sisters would be wearing identical dark green winter coats over identical red velvet dresses, their white tights sagging, but their black patent-leather shoes shiny and new. Her mother would be in full makeup, lips red, not yet taut and strained, a black wool coat with what she referred to as her "fox tails" slung around her neck. Laura, bored with Mass, would stare into the eyes on the face of the fox making up all sorts of stories in her head about him. What he'd seen, where he'd lived, how he'd gotten caught. Sometimes the "he" was a "she" and had several abandoned little foxes stranded in a hole somewhere. Entertaining herself with fox tales got her through Benediction, giving comedy, tragedy, and a whole backstory to that silver-gray accessory. Her father, sitting next to her mother in the pew, resembled the picture of respectability with his dark-navy wool suit and red Christmas tie. Toward the end of Mass, while Laura tripped out on incense and her mother's dead pet, her father's right eye would start twitching, signaling his need for a drink.

When Mass was over, the family got into the car and headed into Manhattan. Because it was Christmas, her dad couldn't pull out his usual line about needing to cash a check on the way out of town. The bank in Sands Point was, for her father, conveniently located next door to Rudy's. Her father underestimated them for years with his check-cashing routine. "Stopping to cash a check," was usually code for downing a quick one at Rudy's. Christmas day he'd drive their wood-paneled Mercury station wagon straight through town and on the Long Island Expressway as far as Queens. He'd then announce he needed to stop for gas. The gas station on Queens Boulevard sat next to an Irish bar called Mahoney's. Her dad would pull the car into the gas station, ask the attendant to "fill 'er up," say he was going to the men's room, while her mother glared at him, saying, "Mike," in a warning tone he paid no attention to. The girls fidgeted in the back while she fumed in the front and Laura's father snuck around the gas station into Mahoney's back door. When he returned, smelling of peppermint Life Savers, his eye would have stopped twitching.

Back on the road, Laura and her sisters would invariably start fighting, grabbing at each other's new dolls while their mother silently blew smoke rings at the closed window.

The Christmas Day when Laura was ten, the family entered the lobby of 1120 Park Avenue after precisely that kind of ride.

"Merry Christmas, Mr. and Mrs. O'Toole, quite a crowd up there already," said Frank, the Irish doorman, looking like he'd been nipping at one of his Christmas bonuses already. Tipping his uniform hat with a swift, yet shaky, hand toward Laura's mother only served to heighten her mom's anxiety. They were late. Her father always wanted her to be the first to arrive, which she never was, and the corners of her husband's mouth were twitching. At that point she, too, would be in need of a drink.

"Merry Christmas to you, Frank, me boy," Laura's father replied, the "me boy" a product of the two drinks he'd belted down back in Queens. While that exchange took place, she and her sisters stood in awe of the gigantic tree covered in silver balls and red lights, dripping with candy canes, and standing in the middle of the white-marbled lobby. After a short elevator ride to the sixth floor, Laura's life would again be grand.

Grandpa Curry's apartment occupied the entire sixth floor. When the elevator door opened into his foyer, they were greeted by laughter, rambunctious cousins, and the sound of the piano playing "Rudolph the Red-Nosed Reindeer." Paula, the housekeeper, was stationed in the foyer, in a fancy black maid's uniform with a white ruffled apron, taking hats and coats and directing everyone into the living room where the party was in full swing. Grandpa Curry was seated in the middle of the room on one of several large, ornate sofas, flanked by two of Laura's younger aunts. As he rose, his portly frame filled the room. Walking toward her mother, arms wide to embrace her, he said, "Margaret" like he'd been waiting days to say it.

"My Margaret's arrived," he continued, a smile spreading across his face, eyes aglitter behind rimless spectacles. Her mother, as his firstborn, still owned that special place in his heart. One arm around her shoulder, her grandfather walked her mother to the couch where her aunts had relinquished their seats. Laura's dad stopped one of the uniformed Irish girls tray-passing cocktails, grabbed himself a highball, and headed toward the piano, where several of the men had gathered, drinks in hand. Within minutes his voice could be heard belting out "had a very shiny nose."

The room, crowded with aunts and uncles, spouses, children, and assorted family friends, overflowed with merriment and sophistication. The grand piano stood at the far end of the room and the Christmas tree, decorated to the hilt and towering over a colorful nation of exquisitely wrapped gifts, stood off to the right by the entrance to the dining room. The women wore satin cocktail dresses, mostly black or red, a few in midnight blue, their arms laden with gold charm bracelets that tinkled and clanked as they gestured. Oversize Tiffany brooches adorned the shoulders of their dresses. Her mother, always the beauty of the tribe, stood out with her dark hair and sky-blue eyes that matched her dress. The men were in their best Brooks Brothers suits and stainless ties. And the monsignors! There were always several, decked out in spotless black with newly starched white collars.

Laura's two unmarried aunts collected priests. Not ordinary parish priests, but monsignors. Two high-caliber, high-pitched ones. Monsignor Brady and Monsignor O'Brien were usually present and accounted for at Curry parties. They were, looking back, and in the words of her cousin Teddy, "gay as a box of birds."

They were probably doing all the altar boys they could get their manicured hands on.

Back then Laura and her cousins just thought they were weird and spoke in women's voices except for Teddy, who all the aunts said, "knew too much for his own good." Monsignor Brady's bald head always looked like he shined it with high-gloss furniture polish, and his heavy handedness with imported aftershave made Laura want to retch.

"Oh, Pat, my dear, you are *so* amusing, do tell that charming story again," he said solicitously to her chubby, wide-waisted Aunt Pat, his ticket to these occasions. He coaxed her, almost seductively, into telling an insignificant story about getting lost by the Spanish Steps when they were together in Rome.

"It's really only amusing if you had been there," said her shy aunt, when no one moved a facial muscle except for Monsignor Brady. He over laughed, whooping like a dying hyena or an old lady you'd expect to be covering her face with a lace hanky.

There were presents under the tree for all The Senator's children and grandchildren. Because there were so many of them, Laura's mother and her siblings worked out a system for gift-giving. Only the godparents gave to their godchildren, sparing aunts and uncles the expense of giving to all the rapidly increasing brood.

Laura's godmother, Aunt Laura, whom she'd been named after, could be counted on for a great gift. She was sophisticated and single. She was desperate to marry and have children, but more than once asked to borrow one of Aunt Pat's monsignors to accompany her to the theater. Laura usually received an expensive and age-appropriate gift from her: a doll from FAO Schwarz with several outfits, or a makeup and vanity set, or a new dress from Best & Co. Her godfather, Uncle Danny, was another story.

Uncle Danny was her mother's youngest and least ambitious brother. He cared about two things actually: horses and playing polo. He, unlike Aunt Pat, verged on obese. Laura always felt sorry for his horses in Quogue. More than a few times she'd seen him head out to the stable on a sweltering summer day in his jodhpurs and high black boots, toting that ass of his. She'd put herself in his horse's place and visibly shiver. She was never terribly proud to be Uncle Danny's goddaughter and least so at Christmas.

Laura wasn't sure whether he didn't know any better or if it was a defiant choice on Uncle Danny's part not to acknowledge the fact that she was a girl. Christmas after Christmas he gave her a variation of the same theme: a toy holster and pistol set, a cowboy hat, and chaps. One year it was red cowboy boots three sizes too small.

CHAPTER 5

The Blind Pony

THAT CHRISTMAS AUNT Laura gave her a beautiful black-velvet jewelry box with a strand of tiny white pearls inside. Laura took the pearls out and immediately put them on. But there was no present under the tree for her from Uncle Danny. Instead, he asked to talk with her "privately" in her grandfather's study. Laura's first thought was money. She thought perhaps he was giving her some and didn't want to do it in front of the other kids. Thinking in terms of several green bills, she followed him into the library.

"I couldn't fit your Christmas present under the tree this year," he said, putting his drink down, without a coaster, on the perfectly maintained, newly polished, well-aged mahogany coffee table. When his drink spilled, he continued, unaware or unconcerned with what was happening to the table.

"I've been watching you over the last few summers and I think you're becoming a good little rider. You deserve your own horse." Her uncle got right to the point. No finessing with "How's school?" or "Are you having a good Christmas so far?" Her mouth opened and she was about to ask him to repeat the last part of what he'd just said (she was also wondering how much he'd had to drink) when he continued.

"Your Christmas present is the sweetest little pony. She's perfect for you. I'll drive her out in a week or two. You have plenty of room on your property and it's 'bout time you had a horse around." Uncle Danny hadn't made it into Fordham or Holy Cross like his brothers, nor did he give a flying fig. He ended up in some college for cowboys in Montana and tried his damnedest to become one. That "'bout time you had a horse around" was his feeble attempt at Hoss Cartwright from *Bonanza*.

He talked about the pony like it was a done deal. Laura's heart raced. She hated all the holsters and cowboy gear but loved riding and horses. The thought of her own pony was overwhelming. It was enough to forgive years of mistrust and disappointment. Laura jumped up and down, then caught her breath. Nothing that great was that easy.

"But what about my parents, what did they say?"

"Oh, they'll be fine," he said, waving his meaty hand like he was shooing away a fly.

Of course, Uncle Danny hadn't cleared his gift with her parents first. His plan was to get her all worked up so they could attack as a team. Her father, for the most part, was no fan of Uncle Danny's. He thought him a "bum," resented her mother for babying him, and endlessly revisited his "fuck-ups."

There was the time Uncle Danny bought an English car, an original Mini Cooper, dark green and in need of many parts and a new paint job, that he left on their lawn for months with the intention of fixing it up but never got around to. There was also the minor, yet explosive, matter of her mother lending Uncle Danny money to pay for polo ponies he bought on credit. Her grandfather refused to pay for them, and when her father found out that her mother footed the bill, he hit the roof. Laura's suspicion, in later years, was that his dislike was more about the food chain. Her Uncle Danny was more of a fuck-up than her father was, so turning around and pointing the finger at his wife's younger brother always gave him a boost.

"Go get your mother and let's talk to her first," Uncle Danny said, knowing full well he could sweet-talk her mom into most things. With her heart damn near racing out of her body and names of horses on her tongue (Honey? Sky? Rocket?), she ran into the living room, grabbed her mother's hand, paying no attention to her protests, and dragged her into the library.

"Well, Danny, that's a generous gift," her mom said, giving her brother a small, strained smile. Excitement was not what she was displaying. Nothing close.

"Please, Mommy, please let me have it, please," Laura cried, trying to interrupt the negative thoughts she could almost hear in her mother's head. "I'm so ready for a pony, pleasssse, Mommy."

"Calm down, honey, I know you're excited, but I can't say yes until I speak to your father." Her tone was gentle, and she kept it that way when she turned from Laura to her brother and said, "Danny, I wish you had run this by me first," knowing full well her brother's strategy: loosen her up with a couple of Manhattans, then go to work on her. She wrapped up the discussion by saying she'd "talk" to Laura's dad during the following week if Laura promised not to nag her to death. She agreed, knowing that promise would be broken by the morning.

True to her word, her mother brought up the subject of the pony the next night before dinner. Taking a cue from her brother, she waited until her father was loosened up before uttering a word about the four-legged gift. Of course, her father's response was a loud—and not unexpected—No!

"You're as crazy as your no-good brother if you think I'm taking in one of his nags. The whole place'll smell like horse shit," he shouted, ending round one.

Not one to drop a subject if it pertained to something she wanted badly, Laura begged, cried, and carried on for the rest of Christmas vacation. She went ahead and told a few of her friends that her cowboy uncle gave her a pony. When school resumed, several asked if they could come by to see it. She explained the pony would be arriving any day and they could come over then.

Her parents fought daily about the pony, which was no big deal since her parents fought daily anyway. The pony just replaced her mother's father and "all his money" as the headliner. Laura, after trashing her first promise in less than twenty-four hours, swore to new promises daily. She'd take care of the pony all by herself. Feed it all by herself, clean its poop all by herself. She'd take care of everything all by herself.

The words, "no good bastard," were heard constantly around her house, both about her Uncle Danny by her dad, and by her mother in reference to her husband.

On a Sunday afternoon, two weeks after Christmas, when Laura's parents were at an impasse and the answer she'd prayed for wasn't forthcoming, Uncle Danny showed up at their house, horse trailer in tow. Laura, outside on the front lawn making a snowman with her friend Irene, had been contemplating whether his hat should go on crooked or straight and if the two different-colored button eyes worked, when she spied a green station wagon desperately in need of a wash coming down the street with a trailer hitched behind it. Running into the house to tell her mother, who was sitting in her blue chair in the living room reading the Sunday paper, Laura unfortunately misjudged her father's position on the living room couch. Thinking he was asleep, stretched out as he was with a section of the paper over his face, Laura whispered too loudly that Uncle Danny and the un-agreed upon pony were slowly but surely working their way up the block.

Lucy, three houses up the street on her friend Helen's front lawn, having bombarded her friend with snowballs, heard the commotion. At the sight of Uncle Danny's car and the horse trailer, she dropped her snowball in the street yelling, "The pony!" and broke into a run.

"Come on, that's my uncle heading to my house and there's going to be fireworks in January!" she screamed back to Helen, running toward her house.

"My pony! My pony!" and Laura was out the door and sprinting toward the trailer with Lucy and her friend and her mother right behind, Peggy bringing up the rear with her swearing father closing in on them. Uncle Danny labored to extricate himself from behind the wheel of his car and greeted Laura with a wide grin, and then walked to the back of the trailer. Her father, thank God, missed one of the front steps in his rage and stumbled, giving her uncle time to unload the pony.

Laura looked at the gift she'd obsessed over continuously for weeks. The gift she'd told her classmates and friends about many times. The gift her parents had fought over since it was offered, and all she could utter was, "Oh." At the same time, icicle tears formed on her cheeks.

"Oh, no," followed by, "Danny, how could you?" Staring at the Shetland pony, wearing a big black patch where its right eye should've been, Laura's mother at once wanted to embrace her heartbroken daughter and slap her thoughtless brother. All she could do, though, was say, "Oh, Danny," reach for Laura, and shake her head.

"You get that broken-down animal off my property right now, you son of a bitch, or I'm calling the cops. Get that fucking pony and your fat fucking ass off this street NOW," yelled her father in his fury. Coming toward them, brushing snow off his pants from his stumble, he continued to yell for the entire world to hear. A small crowd of neighbors had gathered, with Laura crying, her mother shaking her head sadly, and her sisters and the neighborhood girls gaping and bug-eyed.

"Take that pony and leave," said Laura's mother to her brother, voice low, sounding like a ship's captain with laryngitis. She'd never heard her mother sound like that with any of her brothers or sisters before. Uncle Danny packed up his pony, with its one eye and pirate's patch, and stuffed his swollen belly into his car. He was escorted up the block by Laura's dad, who raced alongside the trailer.

"Get that nag the hell out of here, you no-good son of a bitch! Off my block! You should be ashamed, you no-good bum!"

Watching him, his long skinny legs working hard to catch up to the trailer, she knew, whatever it looked like, her father wasn't fighting for her or the real pony she'd been expecting. Not once did he acknowledge her disappointment. He was using that moment, her moment of utter loss and total embarrassment, to solidify his place in the food chain. That's all. He'd be tossing that blind nag at her mom for days, weeks, months to come. It was in his pocket to be pulled out whenever it was needed.

CHAPTER 6

Doomsday

OCTOBER 4, 1963, NEW YORK City. Midmorning, she's in her eighth-grade English classroom at Marymount—an all-girls' school, housed in a white stone mansion on Eighty-Fourth Street and Fifth Avenue. She'd been there for a month and was thrilled to be there. Thrilled to walk down Park Avenue, then over to Fifth, each morning wearing the requisite gray-flannel jumper over the clean white blouse. Ecstatic to pull her knee socks up and out of their squeezed-down positions overlapping oxblood oxfords. Her mother had "suffered a stroke" the year before and needed to work with a "stroke specialist" in New York City. They sold the Sands Point house and moved into her grandfather's apartment. He had died a year earlier. A heart attack in the swimming pool of the New York Athletic Club after his third lap. Her two unmarried aunts who lived with him at 1120 wanted to move into their own apartments. The timing couldn't have worked out better.

For Laura it was a dream come true except for the stroke. Her mother's speech had been affected as well as her hands and legs. The previous year she seemed to get worse. Working three times a week with the "stroke specialist" in New York would heal her. Or so the story went. They packed up the house of shame, packed up the station wagon and Jimmy the gardener's broken-down Ford truck, and, like the Beverly Hillbillies, headed to Park Avenue. To their new clean life. Laura's father promised he'd cut down on the booze; her mother would walk and talk again. The dilapidated "estate" was a thing of the past.

Sitting in English class that morning, Laura was unnerved by the sight of the headmistress at the classroom door, holding her sister Lucy's hand. A red-hot flush crept up her neck, its tentacles heading for her cheekbones. Lucy's face was its usual blank page, always her best defense. Sister Bowman excused the disruption of the lesson, asking Laura to "come along." Her stomach twisted, tightening as it did at times, signaling trouble up ahead, she marched, face aflame, from her desk in the back of the classroom to join them at the door. Lucy took her hand as they walked down the hall to the headmistress's office. That simple gesture unnerved her even more.

Sister Bowman was one cold cookie indeed. A tall, thin, bony woman with a pinched face, so pinched, in fact, that it was understandable why she'd become a nun. There was more than the love of God at play there. Hiding out, wrapped in starched black cotton from head to toe was more the point. Laura had been in her office once before, the day of her school interview. She was scrutinizing her then, and Laura hadn't liked it. That morning the nun oozed pity, and she liked that even less.

"Lucy, Laura," she began, clearing her throat. Why does throat-clearing always mean something bad's coming next, Laura started to wonder, when out it came. "Your mother was taken to the hospital this morning," she continued. On the word *hospital*, Laura's knees began to buckle.

"Your aunt Laura is on her way to pick you up and take you there now. I am so sorry, girls. Come, let's pray together until your aunt gets here."

Pray? Laura wanted to throw up on the spot where the hem of the nun's black habit touched the toes of her black shoes. *Pray?* She wanted to scream. Her worst nightmare had just come true.

Her entire going-to-school life, Laura had been afraid to leave the house in the morning for fear that her mother wouldn't be there when she got home in the afternoon. Or worse, that her mother would need her during the day, and she wouldn't be there to help her. In the third grade, Laura had grown so neurotic about these fears that she devised clever ways to make herself sick. For instance, she drank a concoction of ketchup, mustard, baking soda, relish, and Worcestershire sauce, spiked with whatever other condiments she could find. Her home brew bought her one, maybe two days, if she was lucky, of throwing up. After Laura repeated the self-induced vomiting several times, her mother gave in and let her stay home for the rest of spring term. They watched *Arthur Godfrey* in the mornings and *As the World Turns* at noon, ate cucumber and bacon sandwiches with plenty of mayonnaise and the crusts cut off, and no mention was made of school. The consequence of repeating a grade was well worth it.

Laura knew she shouldn't have gone to school that morning. Her mother had had a cold for the past few days and when Laura kissed her goodbye, still sleeping in what had been her grandparents' four-poster bed, her forehead felt warm.

She knew whatever it was, it was bad. She and Lucy wouldn't have been sitting in that office with those beady, brown nun eyes beaming pity down upon them, if it weren't.

Her aunt Laura arrived within minutes, breathless and visibly upset. She had a cab waiting downstairs and, after a quick word with Sister Bowman about prayer, no doubt, the headmistress walked them to the elevator down the hall

from her office. Students were forbidden to use that elevator. Unless they were rushing to a dying mother.

Her aunt gave instructions to the driver: first stop, East
Eighty-Fourth and Park, St. Ignatius School, to pick up
Peggy, then on to St. Martin of Tours Hospital at Thirteenth
and Sixth. Then she proceeded to tell them her version of
what was going on.

Shortly after they'd left for school that morning, their
mother had been rushed to St. Martin's. Her cold had turned
into pneumonia. She was having trouble breathing.

Laura thought back a few hours to eight A.M. Before
leaving for school, she went into her parents' bedroom, at
the end of the long hallway, like she always did, to kiss her
mother goodbye.

Her mother lay sleeping. Sleep hair, short and brown,
decorated the pillowcase. Her face, half hidden under the
covers, was small, pale, and warm. Laura left for school that
day, the way she'd left for school many a morning, kissing
her mother lightly on her head so as not to disturb her.

Years before, when she was small and didn't understand,
the bed business was all very vague. She caught phrases:
"stomach operations," which in truth were miscarriages,
"colds" and "flu," the akas for overindulgences of Scotch or
gin, depending on the season. These last few years, though,
it was "the stroke" that was referred to daily and blamed
regularly for the debilitation of her mother.

It started by affecting her speech. On good days she
merely slurred her words, so Laura wasn't sure if it was "the
stroke" or the second drink, or both. On bad days, trying to
communicate left her mother exhausted and frustrated, and
Laura in tears with a stomachache. Gradually her mother's
arms and legs weakened. In the beginning, she walked holding Laura's hand, like it was nothing out of the ordinary.
Just mother-daughter affection. Then Laura began, instinc-
tively, cupping her mother's arm firmly at the elbow. That

past spring, her mother had begun to use a walker. How jarring it was to see a beautiful woman with fine features and an elegant thin body, with her coiffed hair and pearls (always the pearls), shuffling down the street or around the house with a metal companion. In the last month, much to Laura's confusion, she had begun to use a wheelchair. That Laura found contradictory. Her mother had been seeing her "stroke specialist" for more than a month, yet instead of getting better she was getting worse.

Laura's aunt left them waiting in the cab while she ran to get Peggy. Laura sat in the cab going over what her aunt had told them. When she was younger, her mother had nicknamed her "my right hand." While Lucy's main function and duty in the family was to look and act like an angel, Laura had become gofer, protector, and nurse, a calling she loved and loathed in equal parts. But it taught her to size things up quickly, and she knew, sitting in that yellow cab listening to the meter ticking, that the situation they were heading into was a lot worse than bad.

Aunt Laura, with Peggy in tow, was back quickly, and the cab headed downtown. Peggy sat in the cab, eyes bulging, barely able to breathe. At ten years old, she looked six, if that. She was short for her age, with a full moon face, and that little pug nose, an extreme cuteness that obfuscated certain anxiety issues about being the baby in the nut house.

Peggy, at that stage in her life, was totally taken with and preoccupied by Jackie Kennedy. She went around the house imitating Jackie all day long. Practicing the First Lady's breathy whisper, "Hello, I'm Jackie Kennedy," or "How nice to meet you; please call me Jackie." She spent hours daydreaming about riding around in limos, smiling, and waving her hand ever so slightly. Pillbox hat pageantry positioned on her impeccably coiffed hair. Laura wished they were rushing downtown in a black stretch car instead of a rickety yellow cab with rotten shock absorbers, just to ease her little sister's pain a bit.

Squeezed between her two sisters, Peggy sitting on the edge of Laura's uniform skirt, Laura heard her heart beating rapidly, thump, thump, thumping like it would beat through tissue, skin, and the breast pocket of her school blouse. Passing through a string of green lights, racing down Fifth Avenue, just past Best & Co., her aunt began to speak again.

"Dear hearts," she began. That was her aunt Laura's expression; she called everyone "dear heart." Laura's father called it "pretentious and theatrical." "Everything is going to be fine," she continued. "Your mother just needs a few days in the hospital, I'm sure, and then everything will be back to normal."

It was on the word "normal" that Laura's anger arrived, pushing up and out of her swiftly. Her feet began to tap rapidly on the cab's rubber floor mat. She chewed on her lower lip, grinding it down until she hit blood, while holding back the words. Bad words, all the four-letter words she'd learned at her father's knee, along with the screams that would cut through the air like flying knives.

She was angry with herself for leaving her sleeping mother, so lifeless in her grandfather's bed that morning. She had known all along that that day would come. Angry at her sisters for being with her, sandwiched between them, on her way to their mother. Her mother was hers. She took care of her. She dressed her and cared for her. She lit her cigarettes and ran her errands. Laura was the only one who knew what she was saying when she slurred so badly that she drooled down the side of her mouth. No one else could help her into or out of bed, holding her so she wouldn't fall. What were they going to do? Sit around the hospital crying like babies? As for Aunt Laura, the sudden venom she felt toward her shocked her. Aunt Laura, sitting there with her signature charm bracelets, their heavy gold's

incessant clicking and clanking. Aunt Laura, with her red
lips and blonde hair, sitting there holding court in the mink
coat Laura's grandfather gave her ten years earlier for her
twenty-fifth birthday, completing her statement to the outside world. Laura's hand wanted to reach across and slap
her.

Aunt Laura had always been the epitome of glamour.
Laura adored her godmother. Aunt Laura had gone to
Yale drama school and worked in "television." She knew
people in "the theater" and even one or two who had gone
off to Hollywood. The friends she brought to the parties
at 1120 Park Avenue when Laura's grandfather was alive
were beautiful, exciting, and in direct contrast to the bald-
ing monsignors Laura's other aunts dragged home. Aunt
Laura was not what one would call a "true beauty." Slightly
overweight, with a few leftover scars on her face from a bad
bout of childhood chickenpox, she had transformed herself
into the "glamorous one" with her clothing, her jewels, and
her expert makeup. Laura was always excited to inhale the
Shalimar scent of her.

Until that day. Until she sat next to her as the cab lurched
its way downtown. With the hot, late-morning sun streaming in on her, Laura wondered why the hell her aunt was
wearing the mink coat anyway. She looked overdone and
vulgar, dressed as she was to see her sister, who was lying
in a hospital bed probably in a thin, white hospital gown
flapping open in the back.

Laura had no memory of entering the hospital. Her
senses were held in abeyance until she crossed the thresh-
old into her mother's room. There, they were attacked from
every direction. Bathed in light from two floor-to-ceiling
windows, the room was blindingly bright, infused with the
kind of filtered brightness that lets you see auras and specks
of dust dance, seemed airless. Somber despite all the light.
There, in the middle of the shimmering white and dancing

dust, lay her mother, her body disappeared under white sheets, framed by an oxygen tent. A clear plastic tent that illuminated yet did not disrupt the incredible tableau of whiteness broken only by brown hair and two liquid blue eyes. Laura was desperate to touch her, but she was under the plastic from the waist up; and from the waist down, there appeared to be nothing. She was afraid that if she touched her mother, she would touch nothing.

Laura looked into her mother's eyes. Guilt and a profound sense of failure swept through her. Her mother was hers, and she couldn't save her. She couldn't keep her breathing of her own accord, couldn't keep her body from melting into nothingness. Chin trembling, eyes welling up, Laura heard a familiar voice.

"Be strong for your mother, girls. She needs your strength. She needs her rest. She's been waiting for the three of you to get here." The voice belonged to the hand Laura suddenly felt on her shoulder. It was then, with the sound of her uncle's voice and the touch of his hand, that she became aware of the others in the room. She turned to face her Uncle Robert, the family elder, standing behind her and saw her father behind him, at the window, dressed in his gray pinstriped Wall Street suit. They looked so sad. So sad, and, at 11:45 A.M. according to the clock on the wall, so tired. Her father, true to form, also looked a little drunk. The corners of his mouth were already twitching. In disgust and resignation, she calculated that by two he would be staggeringly. So she blocked them all out, that small army she realized she in no way belonged to—her father, her aunts, her uncles, her two sisters. None of them existed. She locked eyes with her mother, and in that moment a thousand wordless thoughts passed between them. They were suspended in time and space, encased in the warm white light. Her mother's eyes drew Laura deeper and deeper into their confidence and told her what she already knew.

Before her mother closed her eyes and drifted off, Monsignor O'Brien, the family priest, walked in, white knuckling his bible and rosary as if seeing death for the very first time.

Hours later, in between calls to Campbell's Funeral Home and Best & Co. to order three identical black suits, girls' sizes 8, 12, and 14, Laura and her sisters were told that there had never been a stroke. Their mother, they learned, had been "blessed" and "spared further suffering." Their mother died of ALS, Lou Gehrig's disease, which she'd had for the past several years. "Only the good die young," they were told, before discussion shifted to the ordering of the shoes to go with their black suits, and the whereabouts of their mother's jewelry. Yes, sadly, there was talk of her jewelry. Several aunts expressed concern about her mother's sapphire and diamond engagement ring, and the pearl necklace and matching bracelet her father had given her before he died, all of which seemed to be missing.

But only a small part of Laura listened. The rest of her, the important parts, like her heart and her soul, had left with her mother.

CHAPTER 7

Jelly Donuts and Troll Dolls

AFTER HER MOTHER'S death, Laura entered the valley of lost souls. Lucy went to boarding school, where she found the normalcy and order she had always craved; clad in her blue blazer with the school's insignia on the breast pocket, knee socks, and Weejun's loafers, she felt safe. It was Peggy, of the pug nose, big eyes, and petite structure, who the aunts worried about. Each of them took to mothering her in their own style. Several, being single, were clueless about mothering. Their idea of it went as far as spending Saturdays lunching at Schrafft's, eating grilled-cheese "sand witches," as Peggy called them, followed by scoops of vanilla ice cream on top of scoops of chocolate, and ending with a treasure hunt in the wardrobe department at Best & Co., during which the ever-adorable Peggy made out like a bandit.

As for their father, he dove headfirst into a bottle where he remained for the next five years, with time off for exceptionally bad behavior. At least once a year the men in white coats arrived and hauled him off to Silver Hill in Connecticut to dry out for a month, then sent him back home a few pounds heavier and boasting sobriety. The white coats in Connecticut always did an exceptional job, but the old guy was a hard case indeed, and it fell to Crazy Kate to manage him.

Her father's Irish housekeeper, Crazy Kate was the whistleblower when it was time for the white coats. Kate wore her jet-black hair in tight curls around her face, looked closer to sixty-five than the forty-five she claimed, and had a laugh like a bleating calf that erupted anytime, anyplace. She stooped like a crone. Wild eyed, a raw nerve always on the move. If she wasn't showing off her psoriasis arms, she was bragging about the doctor she worked for in "Wilkes-*Baree*," Pennsylvania.

She lived in and was happy for the thirty-five dollars a week Laura's father paid her, having nowhere else to go. Kate cleaned the apartment, made dinner every night, though not the Julia Child of the Emerald Isle, for sure, and picked Peggy up from school every day. On Saturday nights, Kate bribed Peggy into dancing with her to Lawrence Welk. After Hershey Bars and the occasional Baby Ruth, she and an enthralled Peggy would jig the night away. Crazy Kate and Laura were enemies from the get-go. Laura knew the woman was nuts the moment she met her. Darting eyes scanning left, right, floor, to ceiling constantly, and the shiny black shoe-polish hair told a mad story. Laura let her know she knew who she was, and Crazy Kate retaliated every chance she got.

Listening in on Laura's phone calls so she could report what Laura was doing to her father, searching through the pockets of Laura's clothes for anything naughty or banned, cigarettes, notes passed in school, anything the old witch could bring to her father to confirm what an evil girl his daughter was. Laura had kept sketchbooks since her mother died. Faces, places, the sky, the sea. Her feelings, ripe, raw, uncensored. Searching through Laura's drawer one day, Kate the Loon came across one of Laura's sketchbooks rife with portraits of her father with devil horns, booze dribbling out of his mouth, and other clearly demeaning visual condemnations of the man. The crazy woman literally flew into his room with that treasure.

Never had Laura felt such violation. Never had she had to battle with herself so hard not to rip someone apart limb by crooked limb. Couldn't anyone see how badly she needed her mother?

✍

LIGHT-HEARTED Peggy, with the Best & Co. label crowding her closet, became as popular as a society debutante. Every weekend there were invitations from all the aunts and uncles for skiing, sailing, horseback-riding outings, to which she was a welcome addition.

Laura was another matter. There was her reputation as her mother's right hand, her aunts and uncles having witnessed it several times—as well as "the mouth on her" in relation to the way she spoke back to her father. It seemed a tacit agreement among them, however, that Laura could fend for herself.

And to the outside world, Laura accepted their assessment rather than snub and abandonment. Her grief and loneliness, the depth of which was beyond her years to fathom, she would keep to herself. Whatever good choices she had made in life to that point came from the years by her mother's side; the bad choices would come from the constant pain she felt after her mother's death.

For months Laura spent weekends in her room, watching old movies on television from morning until night, eating jelly donuts she had delivered from Gristedes, New York City's premium market. When she had started eighth grade at Mayfield Hall, she made friends immediately. She was funny and the summer before she'd been social director of her group of friends back in Sands Point. The first day, she walked in buoyed by confidence. These immediate friendships turned out to have a short life span.

She was surprised to find out that New York City girls in her class weren't as sophisticated as she had imagined. They played with Troll dolls, giggled at the very mention of boys, or God forbid, anything sounding the least bit sexual. "Eighth grade and they're all playing with these ugly little Troll dolls. Girls' school, I get it, but tiny plastic dolls, smaller than my palms with rainbow-colored ponytails coming out of the top of their heads?" She reported that over the phone to her friend Nina in Sands Point. The girls named their trolls and had them converse with each other. It was reminiscent of her second-grade Barbie doll tea parties.

After news of her mother's death had swept through the school, she became the most popular girl in her class. That is, for all of five weird minutes. She was a charity case. The mothers of these new "friends" had instructed their daughters to invite the "poor girl" home after school to stay for dinner. It was a pity party Laura quickly opted out of. Between plastic monsters and mindless talk of cotillion dance classes with, of all things, boys, Laura preferred the company of old movies and jelly donuts.

Toward the end of that school year, Laura became friends with Fiona and Sarah, smart rule-breakers a year ahead of her who were always ready for an adventure. Fi had beautiful blue eyes and a scorching sense of humor. Her father had returned to France after Fi's mother promoted herself from a part-time to a full-time lush. Sarah, the more studious of the two, still found plenty of time to cohort with Laura and Fiona. While there were no boozers in her family, Sarah's mother was nuts. Payne Whitney psycho ward twice-a-year nuts.

The summer between ninth and tenth grade, Fiona and Laura hitchhiked from New York City to Sag Harbor, almost at the end of Long Island, and spent five days at Sarah's family's summer house without Sarah's mother even knowing. Her mother had said a definite, rather loud "no" when Sarah asked if she could invite them. Fiona and Laura hid in the closet whenever they heard her footsteps. Sarah pilfered food from the kitchen to keep them alive and nobody was the wiser. Sarah and Fiona were Laura's best friends. They were like the girls she had grown up with in Sands Point. She felt she was her authentic self with those two. They kept her from drowning in the sea of sorrow she swam in daily after her mother's death. Small as it was, they were her tribe.

As the years passed, never budging from gray no matter how sunny, Laura and her sisters chose or fell into what life offered motherless children.

Her father had his own routine. He got up, drank coffee, strong and black, and went off to the New York Stock Exchange where he made hand signals conveying the buying and selling of stock in everything from pig farms to peanuts. At noon his brain flashed "bar open."

At night he sat in his wife's old blue chair in his undershirt with those yellow stains at the armpits working through a bottle, telling himself and anyone who passed through the living room what a fine husband he'd been.

More than once Laura's impulse control failed to kick in. Some snide remark like, "And Crazy Kate is Liz Taylor!" would jump out of her mouth, then they'd be in the ring bouncing each other off the ropes.

Good years?

That would be a lie.

Bad years? That would be true if Laura told anyone the truth. She lived on Park Avenue. True. More details were

irrelevant and unnecessary to the rotten situation she called
her home life.

Finding herself was a search party of one; going forward,
it became a process of elimination. She would no longer be
the rebel girl, the orphan, or the would-be socialite. She
remembered an English expression a friend used to say
whenever she saw someone outrageous looking: "What's
that when it's at home?!" Who would she be, and where
would she call home?

CHAPTER 8

The Little Drummer Boy

THE FIRST TIME Laura got laid was nothing to be proud of. She was seventeen and barely getting passing grades. It was her junior year and she'd been pissing it away since about November. Her ninth and tenth grades had flown by quickly. Her main concerns being if she had enough cigarettes and avoiding her father. She was quieter and kept to herself a lot, listening to Linda Ronstadt and the Stone Poneys' "Different Drum" until the vinyl gave. While most of her friends feverishly sent away for college catalogs and buckled down for SAT prep, she handed in her midterm exam booklets blank as a newborn's ass. Sleeping through breakfast as a regular thing, starting the day off with a Coke and a Hershey bar out of the vending machine, sauntering into class, Coke bottle swinging lightly from her hand like she didn't give a shit, seemed to be her way of dealing with that year.

Her father had moved out of 1120 the year after her mother died. He took a two-bedroom farther down Park with a view of the back of the next building, furnishing it with the dregs of their old house in Sands Point and not much else. It felt cold and run-down, same as Sands Point, except that instead of mice, they had cockroaches. When her father bragged that they lived on Park Avenue, which he frequently did, she always wanted to interject, "Yeah, without any furniture."

The two-bedroom with a maid's off the tiny kitchen was on the fourth floor facing Eighty-Third Street, hence the lack of good light. Laura shared a room with Lucy and Peggy. Lucy refused to speak to their father after their mother died and his cocktail hour moved to noon from five P.M. She told him she'd resume talking to him when he stopped drinking. At night he'd sit on that old blue chair wearing his suit pants and undershirt, whiskey in hand, mumbling conversations with himself to Lucy. If Laura was within earshot of his rhetoric she'd mumble under her breath, "And Santa's calling you tomorrow, Dad."

One night after the Spring Cotillion at the Plaza which she'd been invited to by Danny Harris, a boy she'd dated the previous summer, Laura went with a group to Harper's, an Upper East Side bar frequented by prep school and college kids sporting fake IDs. Eight of them squeezed into one of the red booths in the back, along the side wall, drinking screwdrivers and gin fizzes, smoking Marlboro after Marlboro. The boys, bow ties hanging loose around their necks, tuxedo jackets thrown over the back of the booth, tried to look over-twenty-one and suave. The girls, all barely seventeen, in long dresses, dyed pumps, and beauty parlor hairdos, discarded their white gloves and slouched down into the red leather in what they believed to be sexy positions. By the time the band came on for a second set, Laura and her pals were drunk. Feeling no pain and emboldened by a borrowed black silk empire-waist dress that flattered her and made her feel taller than her five feet four inches, Laura took an unabashed interest in the drummer. Falling more in love by the minute, she sat chain-smoking, drinking from whatever glass her hand landed on, all the while keeping eye contact with that newly discovered loved one.

He had the obligatory long hair and brown eyes, and, to her drunken eye, a poetically chiseled face. Danny's face was lovely, sweet, preppy, and puffy. He was a freshman at Amherst. Laura had gone to his homecoming weekend that past fall. They did nothing the whole weekend except make out. By Sunday afternoon he'd gotten to "third base," his hand over her underpants, not inside. That's all they did, make out, cook cheese fondue, and watch the winter Olympics on his roommate's black-and-white TV. Figure skating, bobsledding, French kissing with cheese breath.

Watching her little drummer boy and the intensity with which he hit those drums made her wet. In all her years as a party-hopping prep-school wild girl, she'd never been wet before. When the band took its next break, Laura wobbled her way past her best friend, Penny, who was making out feverishly with a freshman from Princeton she'd met at the dance, and followed the drummer boy down the burgundy and vomit-colored carpeted stairs to the lounge area outside the bathrooms. The lounge area smelled worse than the bathroom. It reeked of stale puke. Instructions on how to hold one's liquor should've come with those fake IDs. Maybe it was about navigating those carpeted stairs when the fourth rum and Coke hit, and the head started spinning.

Leaning against the wall outside of the men's room, the drumstick hero was waiting for her. No introductions needed. A hot tongue down her throat as he pinned her against the wall did the trick. "That was our last set," he whispered. "Wanna come home with me?"

"Sure," she said, following him out the basement door, marginally aware of leaving Danny and her friends upstairs. Helping her into a cab, her rock 'n' roll hero continued what he'd started outside of Harper's men's room. She was too far gone on rum and lust to pay attention to where he told the cabbie to go. The only thing she could concentrate on was not throwing up. Barfing would've been such a mood breaker. Except for a spinning head and the electric blender threatening to go off in her stomach, she'd never felt so amazing. Hot. She'd never felt that kind of heat. She'd never felt the rush from an exceedingly hard dick pressed up against her thigh before.

The cab pulled up to a bland gray tenement. In her slurry state, she assumed they were somewhere downtown. Musicians and artists were starting to move to the alphabet streets down past Greenwich Village, so when she saw the building, so unwelcoming, so drably uninviting, that's where she told her drunken self she was.

His apartment was a railroad flat. The first she'd ever been in. Dark and cold, it sobered her up a bit. Her new love led her down the narrow hallway into his bedroom. A mattress on the floor covered in tangled sheets and a camel-colored blanket that Bosco, her family's old mutt, wouldn't have slept on served as their love nest. A pink plastic clock radio that belonged in a girl's bedroom and an ashtray with a half-smoked joint sat on the floor beside the bed. The art on the walls consisted of torn covers of music magazines Scotch Taped to various spots, mainly in places that could best be seen from a prone position.

Eric Burden of the Animals stared at her as her lover, no names had been exchanged yet, lit the joint, sucked on it deeply, and put it between her easily parted lips. Her body readily responded to any cue it was given by the guy. Pot smoking was something new to her at that point, having only done it once before. (She said she felt nothing that first time, then proceeded to eat several stacks of frozen waffles.) Adrenaline pumping, she no longer had to throw up. When the contents of the joint hit her, it was all over. Soon she was getting full-on fucked in that pigsty by a nameless stranger she'd known for maybe an hour.

She liked the foreplay a hell of a lot more. The kissing that escalated as she descended into it, and let in every smell, every taste, melted her into the moment. The dried sweat on his body had the whiff of cat food and a shower would have done them both good, but with all she had going on she decided she wouldn't let that be a killjoy. Her breath shorter, her temperature rising, and her heart pounding, she wanted his hands on her breasts that were swelling literally up and out of her. She was completely out of her head in a most delicious and totally new experience.

Until the actual penetration.

And so, it was. Drunk and stoned, Penny's black borrowed evening dress heaped on top of some stray drumsticks on the floor, Laura lost her virginity while her mother shit in her grave. Or so she would imagine later. Sharing a postcoital cigarette with her deflowerer, Laura couldn't tell where he was from by his accent. He didn't have *a dems, des,* and *does* thing signaling Queens, nor did he speak working-class Long Island. She asked and it figured: Jersey. That seemed enough conversation, so they smoked the rest of the joint and fucked again. And once again she enjoyed everything leading up to the entry much more than when he was inside of her grinding away, going from side to side in short jerky motions screaming, "FUCK ME BABY!" at the top of his lungs before collapsing on top of her while she cringed.

She'd made the mistake of opening her eyes for a second during round two and found herself hallucinating. He was middle aged. His long hair dripped grease. He had a small, protruding pot belly; his thin tattooed arms, pale where not brazenly tattooed, stuck out of a stained T-shirt with illegible writing scrawled across the front. His name was Jamie. They exchanged names during the cigarette break. Jamie was the kind of low-rent loser one would regard suspiciously as he parked his beat-up VW bus, a bumper-sticker parade if there ever was one, near a public park filled with young children.

On the other hand, Jamie was a real "let's have a smoke and talk after sex" kind of guy. After round two, he lit up another Marlboro and began telling Laura about himself. At twenty-two, he was in his second serious band. They were about to cut a demo tape. Someone knew someone who could get it played for someone. What about that new band Cream? They had a "dynamite drummer" although, he, Jamie, was better. At that point Laura started falling asleep, lulled by the shame of it all, until Jamie said, "My girlfriend's going to do sixty-nine with me tomorrow night."

"Excuse me?" Laura said. Jamie elaborated on it, that time adding how he was "so excited" about his "sixty-nine" to come, like a little boy talking about the train set Santa's bringing. Like a moron. He was as proud of what was coming as Laura was mortified. There was only one thing left to do. Mumbling something like, "That's nice," she passed out.

She awoke in the morning, her mouth tasting like boiled wool. Sunlight coming from the single window in the room dared her to get up. That was a truly tawdry feeling: waking up hung over as hell, mascara tracks down to your chin, the stench of a smoke-filled beer bar seeping from your skin, finding yourself in some dump you barely remember going to. As you open your eyes, slowly, one at a time, like you're pulling taffy with both hands, you promise God a shitload of things to make it not so bad. Well, God wanted Laura to look at the morning after losing her virginity in bright sunshine, shining a glorious yellow light all over the dump from that lonely, shadeless window. Slapped her in the face with it to pay for her sins. A quick look at lover boy, face pressed into his pillow, rhythmic snoring, coming in intervals, pressed her to get a move on.

Nothing added insult to injury on the mornings after better than having to put on the last night's party frock, she thought, walking out to the street to find a cab. Hailing a cab reeking of old booze and stale cigarettes in the dress from the night before was such an ugly thing. Why not just hold up a sign, TRASH or GOT LAID? She wasn't prepared for the feeling that overcame her when she reached the street. The morning was too warm, too clear, and way too bright. The street was deserted. Laura hadn't a clue where the hell she was in her black pumps, fake pearls, and the borrowed black dress. Looking like the dog's dinner, she walked the empty blocks, one building shabbier and less familiar to her than the next.

As a black-and-white cat slinked out of an alley and meowed its way up to her, Laura became aware that not only was her head pounding but her vagina was throbbing. Crying out its humiliation with every throb. The garbage cans, overflowing from the weekend, began to give off a pungent odor. Overripe bananas, putrefying pears, a baby's stale sun-cooked diapers. Not a clue as to where she was and not a cab in sight, Laura kept walking.

After a few blocks she spotted several people walking into a church. Happy to see that some signs of human life remained the morning after she'd gotten laid for the first time, she prayed it wasn't a Catholic church. That would usher in a realm of instant karma all its own. Hurriedly she approached the first person she came to, an elderly gentleman whose dark suit looked like it had been put in a hot dryer instead of sent to the dry cleaners.

"Excuse me, sir," she said meekly, but with purpose, "could you tell . . ." but he cut her off.

"You, you go 'way, is church, go 'way." He shushed her, waving his hands the way one shoos a dog. "Go 'way, you go 'way."

So she walked away. In her relief at seeing live humans, she'd obviously forgotten what she looked like. Christ, he probably thinks I'm a hooker, she thought. Spying a statuesque black woman in a lime-green hat talking excitedly into the receiver of the phone in a booth at the corner, Laura caught the tail end of her conversation and headed toward her.

"That's right, Nigger, I said I'm changing the lock," said the woman. She slammed the phone down. "And I mean it this time," she said to herself, then waited a few seconds to compose herself and left the booth, smiling at Laura.

"I sure told him, didn't I? These men's is all alike. Every damn one of them," she said to Laura, as if she were a friend or someone other than a pathetic-looking, eavesdropping white girl clueless as to her whereabouts.

"Excuse me," Laura began. What came out of her mouth next surprised the hell out of her. "Why did you call someone a nigger when you yourself are a Negro?" To her even greater surprise, the woman burst out laughing.

"Cuz he's my nigger, girl. And my man. And I can call him whatever I want. He didn't come home last night, so this morning he is my no-good nigger. Besides his smell is gone and that is the beginning of the end. Baby, you look like you got some man troubles of your own."

"Something like that," Laura said, blushing through the last night's makeup. "Do you happen to know what street I'm on? I haven't seen a street sign for blocks, and I'm not that familiar with lower Manhattan." The woman looked her up and down, shaking her head, a benevolent smile spreading across her beautiful brown face before answering.

"Girl, I don't know where you started out last night, but you woke up in Brooklyn this morning—and wearing the Sunday morning blues if I ever saw 'em."

CHAPTER 9

The Irony of it All

LAURA'S FATHER DROPPED dead outside of his happy place. Five years after his wife died. He was standing outside of Tommy Flanagan's pub on Third Avenue and Ninety-First Street. Flanagan's had replaced Rudy's as her father's watering hole when the family moved into Manhattan. He was standing on the street talking to one of the regulars when, boom, down he went. They carted him off to the hospital, then swiftly into the ICU, where he remained comatose for three days before departing.

Alcohol poisoning, they said. After being stone-cold sober for several months, then downing three shots of whiskey at Tommy's. Some of the regulars shook their heads, and one or two said that's why it never paid to get sober.

In a merciful way, it turned out to be a heart attack.

Laura was eighteen at the time and the only one around to get the call. Both Lucy and Peggy were away on a spring skiing trip with an aunt and a few of their cousins. Laura came home to the apartment she shared with a friend on West Sixty-Ninth Street after seeing Peter, Paul, and Mary at Carnegie Hall, and was about to roll a joint when the phone rang. It wasn't that odd for the phone to ring at eleven thirty on a Saturday night back then, so the only thing that surprised her was her uncle's voice. Laura hadn't spoken to that uncle in at least a year.

"Your father's at Metropolitan Hospital in a coma. I'm coming to pick you up. What's your address?"

What a fine howdy-do and how are you. Oh, and how'd you get my number by the way.

She gave her address, hung up, and hurriedly finished rolling the joint. She'd have to be fortified for the rest of that Saturday night.

There was no small talk, just the facts, careening across town and up to East Ninety-Eighth Street in her uncle's station wagon, the SUV of that generation. Just the facts. Her father had been out shopping in thrift stores on Third Avenue for furniture for the new house on Long Island (Really, on Ninety-First and Third?), stopped into Flanagan's to say hello (Again, really?) or cash a check (Oh, please.), must have had a drink or two, and then bam, out cold on the street not ten minutes later. It occurred to her to ask her uncle the source of those facts—the man her father had been chatting with? Or Tommy himself? Surely not from the comatose victim . . . But Laura decided not to. Instead, she rolled down her window to let the March air in and clear the smell of her uncle's son's gym shorts and his two Labrador retrievers, which was making her feel slightly nauseous.

Just when the old man had been looking so good, too, she thought. Three weeks earlier Laura was sitting across the table from him at the Croydon Deli, admiring his tan and listening to his plans. Eating cottage cheese on crackers washed down with Tab, she resisted falling for his story of how different things would be. Different, huh? Splat facedown on Third Avenue wasn't so much different as a change of locale. His face-falling routine was usually in the comfort of his bathroom. And there he was, lying on his back.

Metropolitan Hospital was no place to die.

Most people who die there have no choice, having just been shot in a gang war or as their bodega was being robbed. Being on the edge of Spanish Harlem, it was also the recipient of all the uninsured ill from Eighty-Sixth Street on up.

No place to die. Nor visit.

Walking into the ICU, Laura grabbed her uncle's hand. She didn't mean to. It was a reflex to steady herself, to stop from fleeing the fluorescent-lit room with the orchestra of high-pitched beeping sounds coming at her. She pretended it was Lucy's hand.

Her father lay lifeless and white as the sheet covering his lower half. Not even the florescent lights or the pea-green walls added any color to what could truthfully be called just a shell. What was that smell causing her nausea to return? Chlorine? Well-ripened body odor from the nurse, whose green uniform matched the walls and whose face had the haggard look of someone who had worked three continuous shifts? Or was it death creeping in doing its decay dance?

What did Laura feel, looking at the cadaver called her father? Irony. Yes, how ironic it was that, of his three daughters, it was she, Laura, at his bedside. Not Lucy, his angel, his beauty, his firstborn, and always the light of his life. Not Peggy, his baby, his button-nose toddler, whose cuteness protected her and saved her from his wrath. But Laura, the one who knew him for what he was and by the age of ten could tell him to go to hell and mean it. "I'm sure you'd like some private time with your dad," her uncle said. That was the last thing Laura wanted but her uncle was out the door so fast she suspected he was the one who needed some private time. And perhaps a cigarette.

"Well, Dad, if you can hear me, let me just say that neither of us could've thought this one up," she said, her voice even and steady. "I'm just happy for you that it wasn't your liver. See, I do care." Time and practice wouldn't allow her to take it any deeper. Not there with the nurse whose face had fallen into folds and the green walls were closing in on her.

There would be tears. No one ever accused Laura of being coldhearted. But they would take years to come. More than forty, as luck, or inept shrinks, would have it. At his funeral, which was surprisingly well attended, several people, including two of her mother's brothers and his best marine buddy, Scotty Johnson, spoke of what a charmer her father had been. A smooth talker and swell dancer. Bringer of life to any party. *Who the fuck were these guys talking about?*

CHAPTER 10

Paul

THE DRUMMER BOY episode in Brooklyn put Laura off pursuing sex further, and date rape wasn't a term in use when a couple of years later she met Paul. If it had been, she would have used it to describe her second sexual encounter, her first with him, the man she married at nineteen. He was thirty. Of the two of them, one would think he would've known better. That coupling was at his insistence, for that's what he did. He insisted. She resisted and failed.

It was not a good experience for her again, the sex he insisted on. They had been on three dates. They met up at the wood-paneled bar of the Maidstone Beach Club her family had belonged to since she was a baby. The club where dead fish mounted on shellacked wood decorated the walls. At eighteen, Laura was allowed into the bar; it was a rite of passage Laura had looked forward to. Her father had passed away, heart attack, not cirrhosis of the liver, earlier that year and their membership was paid up through September. Right before he died, her father moved out of the city, back to Long Island, and into a reasonable house, in a good neighborhood, that he again furnished with the dregs from Sands Point. That was where Laura and her sisters lived through the summer while aunts and uncles decided on their fate. Having the beach club that summer was one of the last links to their fast-vanishing past. A last hurrah to the pool, and the ocean their mother loved so dearly, and to the white-sand dunes. And to their youth.

Laura was in the bar with a girlfriend, sitting on a club chair, screwdriver in hand, about to start a game of backgammon while pretending not to notice the group of men at the other end of the bar loudly playing liar's poker like they owned the place. Clue One, not heeded: She recognized one of the three guys. She'd seen him around the club for years and his reputation preceded him. Paul Hayes. Vague as the details were, she remembered hearing snippets of the story over the years. He'd been involved in the debutante party in Southampton that made the news when a bunch of preppies got drunk and trashed the place. One guy totaled his car at four in the morning, almost killing his date in the process. Photos of the trashed house next to a picture of his date in her hospital bed were all over the Long Island newspapers.

Paul Hayes was the one who approached her, the celebrity bad boy, saying he could tell she needed help with her backgammon game. She really didn't, which would've been Clue Two, had she not been so flattered to be noticed. Paul Hayes, hitting on her, so much older that he could rightfully be called a man. Physically he wasn't impressive, on the shorter side, but with a fine body, although a bit too muscular in the chest. His black hair was thick and a source of pride, his beseeching brown eyes something she couldn't figure out. He didn't smile widely or laugh with his mouth wide open, she noticed. Two screwdrivers later, Paul walked her out to the parking lot, kissed her with a roving tongue, then asked her out for the next night. Too worked up to notice the roughness of his tongue, she said yes, missing Clue Three.

The next night they drove out to the other end of Long Island for a party where Laura got drunk, threw up, and passed out, handily circumventing any postcoital mortification, let alone the act itself. The next day, which officially could be called their third date, is when it did happen. The sex.

They drove back to Manhattan after waking up in Long Island, hung over from the party, and went straight to Paul's apartment. It was a small one-bedroom in a well-appointed brownstone off Fifth Avenue and East Seventy-Third Street. Impressively grown-up, well furnished with the castoffs from his parents' Locust Valley estate. The idea was to rest up a bit, and then go to a movie and dinner. Naive. Hung over. Swept away by attention.

As soon as she lay down on the bed for a "rest," Paul was on top of her. He had a hard boxer's body as well as a hard-on. Every time she said, "Wait," he smiled and mumbled, "You don't mean it." That's when she noticed his rotten teeth. She'd never seen such bad teeth on someone who could afford a dentist. As she started to think how traumatized he must have been by some dentist, he pinned her to the bed with one arm, while the hand of his other arm ripped open her blouse. He was going to get what he had planned on last night before she'd thrown up and zonked out.

"Wait," she tried to say, before he rammed his tongue down her throat, choking her, his cock slamming away inside of her.

A year later they were married. It made no sense and total sense. He had an MBA, she barely made it out of high school. His mother went on a rampage when she heard the news. Seriously shaken, she feared being deleted from the New York Social Register. Paul's mother calmed down when she found out that one of her closest friends had also been a friend of Laura's grandfather.

For Laura, marrying Paul was an act of desperation. Her father had died almost a year earlier making her officially an orphan. Tough as she thought she was, the reality of that left her lost, anchorless, and afraid.

A girl desperate for a home. Add to that having a thirty-year-old, educated man of means want her, the girl whose father told her repeatedly during her formative years that he'd seen bad kids before, but she was the worst, and you had a girl who knew only one thing about love. And that was how to spell it.

They stayed married for five long years. There were fun times with Paul. He loved Formula One car racing and they went to tracks all over the country. They could both listen to Tim Hardin's "Misty Roses" for hours on end. For a week every winter, a trip to the Bahamas was a given. A house in Southampton every summer, another given. She got to play grown-up inviting people for cocktails. He could make her laugh. His commentary on certain people, although full of judgment, would usually leave her bent over, clutching her sides, begging him to stop. And his friends . . . well, two really . . . the others were as flatly ironed as his shirts. His best friend, John Broad, was an ivy league elitist gone bad. At some point, he sported the same khaki pants, buttoned-up shirt costume as his frat brothers at Yale. At six foot four, he towered over those bros. When Laura met him, his daily outfit consisted of black leather pants that were tight enough to work, and a tan, fringed leather jacket. He went from selling pot in the dorms to flying small Cessnas of it in from Miami.

Dangerous. From his low Texan accent to the way he looked into her eyes like he saw something he knew in them. That kind of dangerous. John was much more alluring to her than his Turnbull & Asser shirted pal.

Robert, the other friend, was from Palm Beach and was the most self-indulgent, spoiled, childish man Laura had ever met. His saving grace was that he was also the wittiest man she had ever met. His face bore that soft puffiness of the upper class. But he made her laugh all the time, even at his own expense. Robert and John were household fixtures, which made living with Paul much more bearable.

Sex with Paul, without pot—a hard, no pun intended, task. She called in sick as much as she could. With enough pot—she could have sex with a goat and feel like she was a Playboy Bunny.

When she divorced him after five years (it took her that long to grow up), Laura left empty-handed, but not empty-headed. Not only could she spell love, but she knew that it was never what she felt for Paul.

CHAPTER 11

After Paul

DIVORCING PAUL TOOK guts. She knew what she had wasn't love, but in many ways it was comfortable. She wasn't heartbroken at all, but she was lost. With money her father left her, she rented a studio apartment in Gramercy Park that was nothing to brag about except for a large window overlooking the park that filled it with light. Asking herself, who she was in heart and soul and what she wanted to do occupied her days for several months. She knew, she had always known, that she wanted to be a painter. Notebooks full of sketches got her through most of her childhood and teenage years.

Attending New York City's prestigious Arts Students League took guts as well. Once again, she was that girl pulling up her knee socks, walking into her new school before her mother died. Wearing jeans, no flare, no bell bottoms, no stars embroidered on the back pockets, and a gray pullover, she entered the building with her shoulders straight back, posture that signaled a confidence she didn't own.

Fifty-Seventh Street, she thought, walking up to the front desk to sign in, it's not uptown or downtown. Neutral territory. Ten minutes early for her first class, figure drawing, a requirement course for all new students, she studied the student bulletin board that was crammed with flyers fighting for space. Laura was mesmerized. One could be the roommate of a guy in Hell's Kitchen or buy a used easel. There were two bikes for sale and a yellow VW Beetle only lightly dented on its front end. Concert tickets and food co-ops ruled, but the main attractions were gallery shows and help-wanted ads.

Laura instantly fell in love with bulletin boards. From that day on she read every one she came across.

You never knew what you can find was a thought that appealed to her. As students filed into their studios, juggling paint boxes, pencil cases, and blank canvases, Laura felt that too-familiar tightening below her ribs followed by the cramping in her lower abdomen that signaled fear. These people in berets, overalls, and capes—capes!—looked like artists. She looked like, felt like, the girl who just took the train in from Long Island.

The Briarcliff College grads Paul's friends had dated were wealthy, sophisticated, but had been easy to crack. She knew the language and the dress code. The sight of a caped girl shuffling down the corridor made Laura fear, with each gut cramp, that she was wildly out of place.

The first assignment in her drawing class was to draw herself.

Her "essence," the teacher called it. Use black or colored pencils. Go for truth not beauty. She couldn't grasp her loneliness which was her truth. She couldn't see its color or shape.

Write what you know. Paint what you need to express. Play the music inside. Mark Twain said the first. The other two were just common sense.

Chaos? Documented in oil a hundred times over. Anxiety? As common on canvas as the black paint used to depict it. Loneliness? That's my truth, but what's its palette? Buffering myself with girlfriends, making out with boys in the sand dunes of the beach club, fashioning that Lilly Pulitzer lifestyle with Paul?

All of it was a ruse, a cover-up. The truth was what she despised.

"Laura, you've been frozen in front of your sketchbook with the tip of your pencil in your mouth for over an hour. You made one small stroke with that hideous green pencil. Is it vomit you are trying to express? If so, you have forty-five minutes of studio time left today. Let the retching begin."

Not one to coddle, her teacher eventually made her, made all his students, face the truth. Laura was the lonely lost sparrow. The no-nest orphan she knew would be pitied, so she hid that bird so deep she forgot it was even there.

The cape girl had the designated space next to Laura's in her painting class. She raced her brush across her canvas like the devil was chasing it. Her hair, a cross between ringlets and unleashed cornrows, looked like it would break a hairbrush. Under her cape, she wore a red-checked vintage dress with holes and stains, and scuffed black boots. The best thing about her, Laura decided, was her low, creamy, butterscotch voice, and her fearless approach to the canvas. She'd stand in front of her easel, layering on pastel colors with swift strokes, making lines like waves of electricity. The lines were mesmerizing. Kind of like her hair. Like her. Her name was Agnes, and her favorite topic of conversation was "balling."

"So, Laura, are you into balling? Balling is my favorite thing to do. See that cutie pie over there painting that red skull, I balled him in the bathroom on the third floor. No one ever uses that bathroom except to ball and smoke pot."

"Thanks, Agnes. I'll keep that in mind."

Laura couldn't bring herself to add, "Next time I need a place to ball."

Amused by the balling talk and soothed by that melting butterscotch voice, Laura was temporarily relieved of the knife-throwing contest in her stomach.

❧

ONE DAY, after two weeks of the occasional balling commentary, Agnes switched topics. "Hey, do you want to go across the street to The Greeks to buy me a cup of coffee?" The Greeks was the designated home away from home for many of the students.

The owner was half Jewish and half Puerto Rican, not a drop of Greek blood in his body or a Greek dish on his menu. From ten to noon and three to five, the place was filled with Leaguers. Noon to two, the place was reserved for the lunch crowd, salesgirls wearing red nail polish and four-inch heels, and elderly antique dealers sporting striped ties and too-small suits who worked in the various shops along Fifty-Seventh Street.

"Love to buy you coffee and split a bagel if you'd like," Laura said, sweetening the pot.

Laura's social life at that point consisted of classes Monday through Friday, then music bingeing. From the time she got home, deli sandwich, tuna, or turkey on rye, in hand, she'd played Jimi Hendrix and Richie Havens on the small stereo she'd bought herself as a divorce present, until "All Along the Watchtower" for the fourth or fifth time signaled bedtime. It was a formative if lonely time for Laura, and The Greeks was a welcome invitation that turned out to be a haven. As much as she felt an outsider at the Maidstone Beach Club in Easthampton was how instantly at home she felt at The Greeks. Between the discussions on art theory and the immature yet passionate critiques (Is Jackson Pollack a genius with all that splash and splutter, or is it the emperor's new clothes?), friendships were formed, romances were started, and a hell of a lot of pot was sold. True generosity was displayed at The Greeks.

"Hey, man, can I bum a smoke?" was never met with a "No!"

"You gonna finish that bagel?"

"It's all yours, pal."

In all their different shapes, sizes, and speech patterns, swilling back lukewarm coffee and bumming Marlboros, that was Laura's tribe.

She went out on a date with one of her fellow students, Joe, a six-foot-tall, sandy-haired guy who looked malnourished in a sexy way. The Greeks felt like a reality check into her life as an artist, and it didn't stop there.

They went on to a Chinese place on the West Side for cheap chop suey and slid into a sticky booth with a green linoleum table and the faint smell of stale soy sauce. Laura had a ginger ale and barely touched her vegetable fried rice. It was a combination of first date eating and not being able to tell what the crispy brown things in the rice were. Crushed cockroaches from the kitchen?

Laura would bet the farm on it.

When the check came, Laura sat there demurely, sipping what was left of her ginger ale, thinking about what would come next.

"Your half of the bill is eleven dollars," was not the what-came-next she was expecting.

"Oh," escaped from her mouth just as a shocked expression arrived on her face.

Not one to miss much, Joe, without the slightest embarrassment, said, "Get used to it, Uptown Girl, that's the way we struggling artists do things."

Joe didn't become her boyfriend, but six months later her life-drawing teacher did. Sam Carr, thirty-two, medium height, medium build, uniform of faded jeans and white T-shirts. Baggy sweaters in winter. Handsome? Almost. Sexy with an irreverent sense of humor were the attributes that hooked her. And kindness. There was always kindness in his critiques and in his advice to his students. Even to the least talented and most annoying of them. Kindness was not a word Laura had ever used to describe men in her life. Every time she thought of Sam's kindness, she felt the stain on her heart fading, replaced bit by bit by the thought that her life could be good.

CHAPTER 12

Leaving the Rabbit Hole

LAURA HAD STARTED to go down the rabbit hole. The small success she experienced: two sold-out gallery shows. Known galleries? No, but official galleries, not some warehouse space that a bunch of artists pitched in for and called a gallery for one night. Still it was not enough. The vast amount of pot she smoked had begun to affect her thinking, fueling her with a new and inflated sense of herself as herself. She wasn't quite waking and baking, but her cocktail hour had been getting earlier and earlier. She put her foot on the accelerator and stayed in fourth gear for too long and too hard. No more nights at home spinning Richie and Jimi. She had a boyfriend and a raging social life. A couple of nights a week she frequented CBGB's, the music bar down in the Bowery, with a couple of friends. The music and the camaraderie of misfits inspired her. Some nights it was the famed Max's Kansas City. Mingling at Max's with Andy and his crew, Brice Marden and his gang, and the art groupies, one more exotic looking than the next, most of them tall Twiggy imitators in two inches of black eye liner, Laura felt like a wannabe around this crowd. A plain Jane from Long Island pretending to have been invited to the party. Sam stayed in and painted weeknights. They were living together in his apartment, using hers as their shared studio. On weekends he partied, pale partier that he was. Monday through Friday nights, he was in the studio in paint-splattered overalls with classic Miles Davis and Thelonious Monk for company, usually heading back to his apartment before midnight.

Sam was the one who pulled the plug on her shenanigans, one night when she came home red-eyed and wobbly. It wasn't a first, a second, or even a third time and it was moving toward becoming habitual.

"The art scene in LA is starting to heat up," he said. "There're these guys in Venice, near the beach, getting big-time attention. Some nut job named Moses, and this guy Ruscha, who apparently looks like a movie star, and a few other guys doing their own thing, which you know is right up my boulevard. So, I'm going, and I want you to come with me."

It took less than half a second for the voice that always saved her to say, "I'll go get packed."

They would spend the next two years living in a loft off Main Street in Venice, the epicenter of all things cool.

CHAPTER 13

Knocking Back Beers at Barney's

IT WAS THE surfer chicks.

Their long blonde hair hitting the top of their string bikinis was irresistible. The art groupies, much more exotic looking. More black eyeliner and faux fur vests, worn over jeans that would fit a long-legged thirteen-year-old, couldn't go unnoticed either. And one day Sam stopped resisting.

No one paid more than seventy-five dollars a month for a cavernous space to live and work in, furnished from thrift stores and street-found throwaways. It was a community fueled by electric energy, both raw and polished talent, competitiveness, and kindness. And there were eager young girls everywhere.

People wandered in and out of each other's lofts any time of day or night. Grabbing a beer or pouring themselves a glass of Lancers rosé or Gallo three-dollar-a-gallon red. Bartering each other's paintings became a game.

"How the hell did you get him to let go of that one?"

"Wait a minute, I offered two of my best pieces and the son of a bitch wouldn't budge."

"What . . . did ya give him your old lady for the night?"

Sometimes it felt like life being lived at the speed of light.

Laura, inspired by the constant sunshine and blue waves, began water coloring, which she found much more challenging than she'd thought. The art scene was such a boys' club at that time. It was hard for her to be taken seriously. Their neighbor, Larry Bell, among the chief officers of the boys' club, who was fast gaining gallery attention for his own watercolors, was an exception. Larry almost regarded her as a peer, respected her work, and admired her sense of color.

Sam was experimenting with layering oil paint an inch thick on canvas, called impasto. Their loft took on that smell, that pungent, toxic, fuming scent that seeps into walls, clothing, skin, hair. It was a smell that brought no joy into her life.

He was also experimenting with the groovy surfer chicks and learning to get those tight jeans off the art groupies in record time. That stopped the flow of joy in Laura's life.

Taking a gallery job on La Cienega that came with a tiny apartment upstairs was Laura's non-bitter, non-resentful nod to moving on.

And how rapidly she moved on.

On Monday nights in the late seventies, the galleries on La Cienega opened their doors and it was party time. Everyone from serious collectors, date seekers emanating Jean Naté and Eau Sauvage, and of course, the Venice bad boys, Ed Moses, Ron Cooper, DeWain Valentine, Billy Al Bengston, and the Dill brothers, Guy and Laddie John, those Malibu-blond surfers turned serious artists, swarmed the block.

She was right there with them, Laura was. In the right place at the right time and ready to kiss Sam and those catalytic surfer chicks for pushing her into the fun zone.

Thinking she'd stay in the zone for a while, playing with some random bad boy sporting tattered overalls, charcoal under his fingernails, with that can-you-pay-for-dinner look in his eyes, she was surprised one Monday night when she couldn't look away from what seemed to be a good guy in a starched white shirt, immaculate jeans, and a navy-blue sports jacket. He stopped pretending to be immersed in one of Valentine's smaller sculptures.

"Hey, umm . . . hi, do you mind if I ask your opinion on this sculpture I'm interested in? Oh, my name's Ben, by the way." He said that as a rushed run-on sentence which Laura found charming. What he didn't say was, "I'm going to be your second husband." What she didn't say was, "God you're cute and those blue eyes of yours are mesmerizing."

Forget play time with broke bad boys. When life gifts you gold, you take it straight to the bank.

CHAPTER 14

Shrimp Sauce

PEGGY WAS GOING deaf. She'd lost 50 percent of the hearing in her right ear and had nerve damage. She was waiting to be scheduled for her third MRI to find out the origin of the nerve damage, and if the cyst found on her brain had grown. It hadn't.

She told Laura all of that on the phone the other night. Single, a tennis coach, Peggy was living in New York City. Laura lived in Los Angeles with her second husband and their baby, Grace. That news wasn't their initial bit of business. First, she gave time to the temperamental Irish guy upstairs. Too much goddamn time, considering the new information. In the five minutes they'd wasted chatting about him, Laura learned enough about him to begrudge the loss of those five minutes.

She was cleaning up the baby's room as they spoke, the portable going out of range once or twice, but Laura stayed with her sister, which wasn't an easy task. Peggy could be an irritatingly slow talker, as if she thought out each word trying to say it correctly. But Laura hung in through her story about the Liam Neeson look-a-like from upstairs who came down to fix Peggy's VCR and asked her out for a drink. "I said 'Okay,' then told him to give me ten minutes to get out of my sweats," Peggy went on. "His girlfriend is about twenty years younger than he is. Sweet, but very dumb. She's in Kentucky visiting her family." Each sentence felt like it took five minutes to follow the one before it, that last in keeping with Peggy's usual penchant for sharing information with which one can do absolutely nothing.

She droned on about the call she got the other morning when the hot water was off in her building and Liam the Lover from upstairs, having no hot water, woke her, screaming "goddamn, motherfucker, cocksucker" into the phone.

Laura began to feel sad. Liam the Lover sounded a bit like Paul, her rotten first husband. When they got to the part when Peggy said, "He's got an Irish temper, but I like to fuck him anyway," they had a laugh and Laura said, "Yeah right, we don't marry Irish guys. Fuck him, send him back upstairs, pick up the phone and order a pizza."

They chuckled a bit more about that. That was new for them, that risqué banter. Very grown-up. They nursed the moment, then—*wham*—came the deaf stuff. Peggy launched into it like she was telling Laura some banal diatribe about returning a pair of shoes to Bloomingdale's or jeans to the Gap wherein the salesperson was rude and unhelpful.

There was slight change of tone, no more. Then came the commentary about the cyst and the MRI she had on Laura's birthday.

"They kept me waiting for an hour and a half," she said, and Laura thought about the roses in the cobalt blue vase Peggy had sent her that day. They must have cost a hundred and fifty bucks. A hundred and fifty bucks Peggy couldn't afford.

Peggy also told her about the incident that prompted that last round of testing. "I was walking down Columbus and Seventy-Fourth, when—this is the way I described it to the doctor—it felt like cement was pouring down from the top of my head into the right side of my face and filling up my ears."

Laura pictured that and caught her breath. *Cold January morning . . . noisy New York City street . . . sun shining . . . wind blowing . . . people rushing . . . boom boxes blaring . . . construction workers wolf-whistling, "heeeeey baby" . . . time to pop into Starbucks for a cappuccino? decaf or regular? . . . Oh . . . Thick sludge oozing downward from Peggy's brain, turning her face to stone.*

Recovering, Laura shot questions. About Peggy's doctors, her diagnosis, her health plan, the prognosis. Peggy told her about her client, the seventy-five-year-old Jewish doctor she coached, who, "as luck would have it," was an ENT. When she told him about her episode at Starbucks, he'd put down his racket, got on his cell phone, and set up a pro bono appointment with a colleague at New York Hospital. "A terrific neurologist," said her ENT.

Well, I should hope so, Laura thought to herself and then thought for a moment about the niche Peggy carved out for herself as a tennis coach to mainly older, and mostly Jewish it seemed, professionals. What a blessing, Laura had thought many times, that her sister gave up acting and lucked into that. She couldn't have tolerated seeing Peggy, gray haired and shrinking, doing dinner theater in Delaware. Her clients loved her and provided her with enough character studies and drama. Laura had heard about the seventy-year-old therapist who had gained so much weight she waddled up to the net like a stuffed duck. The retired gynecologist who invited Peggy to Westhampton for the weekend, with the idea of a ménage à trois with his agoraphobic wife. And there was Marge Finkelstein, on the board of Lincoln Center, who had lent Peggy the black velvet skirt and navy-blue satin jacket she wore to Lucy's daughter's wedding in November. Caroline Herrera. It complemented Peggy's large and lovely eyes.

Those baby blues don't see well enough, even with glasses on, to catch their own sadness. Her clients had bequeathed her cash, two-carat diamond stud earrings, and a Cartier Tank watch. Gifts from the living? Free medical attention.

When Peggy launched into another tale about another nice Jewish man, Laura began to wonder whether her sister mentioned "Jewish" in her stories to connect with her, married to a nice Jewish man, or because they were sitting in the lap of their latest rapprochement or both. Or because she was unconsciously parroting their past. "Nice Jewish . . ." being straight from the mouths of any one of their aunts.

Anyway, the nice Jew from New York Hospital had confirmed the 50 percent hearing loss in the right ear as well as the nerve damage. By that time, Laura was downstairs sitting on the living room couch. Ben walked past her on his way into his office and looked at her with concern. She mouthed, "Peggy." She shook her head, letting it all sink in from one side of her own ear to the other, as if trying to shake it away.

BUT IT stuck. For days Laura thought about her little sister while driving in her car, a fully loaded Jeep Cherokee with front grille, CD player, and Dolby sound and speakers, Peggy memories piling in and out of her mind and heart faster than she could sort through them.

Peggy, the most adorable baby ever born, got the short end of the stick. Laura once described it to her shrink: Lucy was born when their parents were healthy and happy. The window was wide open. By the time Laura came along, a year later, the window had closed considerably. But Peggy, coming along three years after that, barely made it through at all. Slipped right through a crack. Squeezed through the thin line of light that the war-torn territory of their parents' marriage had left.

She thought about it, sitting out by her pool, watching the LA winter sun reflect aqua crystals off the water. Sitting on the rubber ABC matting that covered the concrete decking around their pool, the bright blue, orange, and yellow squares cushioning her while she built a Lego house with Grace, who, at two and a half, was happy, healthy, and heard everything perfectly. She and Ben had been married for almost four years that Laura could only describe as blessed. If she believed in perfect, she would have used that word instead. Marrying Ben for her was winning the lottery. The big one. The million zillion one that kept on giving. She wanted her sister to have a husband who adored her as well. She wanted her to have a freckled-face toddler with red-apple cheeks instead of a vat of cement filling up her ears.

She saw Peggy when she was little. Talk about cute. Peggy was the original button. Pug nose, cupid mouth, big eyes. She was always asking them to repeat things. "What?" Peggy would say, or "What was that?" or "Tell me again!" And Laura and Lucy would berate her.

"Well, if you'd pay attention," Lucy would say.

Laura would shut her up with "What are you, dumb?" Laura had no time to repeat herself.

Like homing pigeons, Laura's thoughts of Peggy flew off, returning with new messages, written from memory or imagination. She saw Peggy at age five, so small they called her "Shrimp Sauce," crashing into the parking meter while running down Central Avenue in Sands Point. Her head was turned, looking behind her as Joey Cittadino from across the tracks, her first crush (he was six and a half), chased her up the street. Smacked right into that damn meter, profile first. Lucy and Laura heard the whack half a block down the street, where they had stopped to watch some prepubescent hoodlum boys from the Catholic school play kickball. That could've done it, smacking into that meter.

She thought about the nerve damage. Maybe it had been there since birth, deteriorating slowly as those deteriorating things do, slowly and silently until the silence was all that's left. And she thought of a woman, her little sister, who, though no longer a girl, bore a slight resemblance to the petite pug-nosed, big-eyed girl she was, sitting alone in a cold fluorescent-lit room in a white gown tied in the back, flipping through back issues of *People* and *Met Home*, or worse, *National Geographic* while she waited to tuck herself into a bed of steel to be slid through a machine that would X-ray her brain. She pictured Peggy later that day, in the one-bedroom walk-up on West Eighty-First Street that she'd lived in for fifteen years. It was decorated in Amish quilts, Moroccan throw pillows, and pictures of Lucy's two kids.

No husband, no boyfriend (that week), no children, no pets. No one to hold her left hand when, with her right hand, she held the phone to her good ear to hear the clinical words for getting the rawest deal in town.

Just imagining it cracked Laura's heart into a million minuscule pieces.

CHAPTER 15

No Legacy

SEARCHING FOR HER mother's legacy was a futile exercise. Her extremely thin wrists, an addictive personality that she struggled to contain with too many Coca-Colas, and her sharp tongue were pretty much it. Her mother died. It wasn't the woman's own jones for the whiskey, or those fucking gin martinis that made her mean as hell at times that did her in. It was a disease no one really knew much about or how to cure.

Laura had lived so much of her life trying to excuse her mother for dying young. For drinking too much. For having a bitch of a temper and the heart of a saint. None of it made her a bad person, or a bad mother. It just made her so much harder to see objectively. Hence, Laura's fascination with shadow and her fear of the fog.

"That's what I came here to paint," Laura thought to herself, driving on old Route 25, the back road from Quogue to Bridgehampton, bypassing the Thursday night traffic. Black and more than a bit eerie, the silent moonlit miles of potato fields, stretching smooth like still waters into a Magritte sky, were an awesome tradeoff.

Laura was staying in her girlfriend's guesthouse, the mini-me of the brown-shingled, white-porched main house. She had stayed there for the two-week duration of her painting workshop, which was ending the next day. It was the first time she'd been there alone. As much as she loved Ben and being with him and as much as she adored Grace. It was all hers: her books, her paints, her music, and her memories.

From the moment she read the invitation, saw the names of the painters, sculptors, and photographers gathering to teach the workshop, she knew that she had to go even though the thought of it petrified her. It read like an index of *Art in America*.

Her pen shook as she wrote her acceptance letter. She would be honored to join "the select group of artists" for the two-week summer program.

The irony was that she had been invited based on the success of her last show, "The Missing Mother: How to Capture her Effect on Canvas." That Laura should be invited to participate in a workshop titled "Investigating Shadow in Fog," was proof to her that a highly intelligent creative force with a hell of a sense of humor was indeed running the show, especially given that Quogue was the landscape for so many of her memories of her mother.

She'd done well. Thrown herself into the program from the get-go. Attended every lecture, mingled with students and faculty members, sought advice from painters she admired. Not knowing at first where the title of the workshop would lead her or what medium she would choose to get there, her use of watercolor and ink felt right. She'd finished three canvases and could see a series taking shape. Back roads stretching into the horizon: multiple shades of black, white, a touch of faded pink here, indigo there, on smaller canvases than she'd worked on before, inviting the viewer in close to follow the road. She felt good, but not ready to head home.

And not ready to head to Peggy's fiftieth birthday dinner either.

She and Lucy were hosting a party for Peggy at the Sands Point Yacht Club. Technically Lucy was hosting, Laura reimbursing. That Lucy and her husband should buy a house and raise their kids in Sands Point still boggled Laura's mind.

One runs from the scene of the crime and doesn't pitch a fucking tent.

"But the schools . . . and there's the yacht club," Lucy had said, regarding settling there. Just a year between them, they had always been worlds apart. Whatever floats your boat, Laura said after the yacht club remark, not oblivious to her pun. But Lucy was right. Both of her boys, fourteen and sixteen, were addicted to sailing, much better than being city crawlers addicted to anything or everything else. The pace of life there was good for Lucy. No New York City social who's who and what are they wearing. Lucy was happy sporting her ten-year-old Gucci loafers and just-as-old cashmere cardigans around town. Robert, her exceedingly handsome husband, got to be the Dr. McDreamy of Long Island with a line around the block to see him.

How perfect that Laura would be in Long Island that summer, Lucy had said. How perfect that they could all celebrate Peggy's big birthday together! And how perfect would a dinner at the club be on a late July night? Pretty damn nice. Of the three of them, Lucy was and always had been the nicest. Laura was beginning to realize that unbeknownst to her, Lucy had always known what was best for herself and had no qualms about doing it. Laura had realized sometime in her late twenties (after she realized why it took her five years to leave Paul, let alone marry him), that Lucy had been not only brave, but true to herself by staying under her bed and then not speaking to her father years later. Laura wasn't brave at all. She was brazen. Different country altogether. She was a brazen little girl, a brazen and rebellious teenager, and a brazen, totally lost orphan when she married Paul. What she and neither of her sisters knew back then was that alcoholics like their father don't stop drinking because they love someone, no matter how large a love it is. They stop when they stop hating themselves and kissing the gutters they fall into.

And on the eighth day, god said enough resting and created therapists.

After her divorce from Paul, it was Lucy that Laura turned to for advice. Her radar for what was right and wrong was never mottled or gray. Laura's would switch palates and dip into gray upon occasion. Not a pure color period. Never a Lucy color.

Long ago, Laura began to respect the little girl hiding under her bed begging her younger sister to "stop them." Lucy had known it wasn't her job.

Writing out Peggy's birthday card the day of the dinner, yet again she saw little Shrimp Sauce in her mind's eye. Her younger sister was happy. She'd married a sweet man two years earlier. Al, a widower, with a waistband as big as his smile. A musician who needed a day job, Al got into sound engineering and installation early and his business grew as his musical aspirations died. His only child was grown and out of the house, so he and Peggy, whom he called My Little Angel, traveled, and had a good life. His engagement present to her had been a top-of-the-line hearing aid. Laura, clueless at that point as to how valuable a man who could deal with a wife's maladies could be, looked past his wide girth, thinning hairline, and loyalty to Crosby, Stills, and Nash T-shirts and saw him as an answered prayer.

Putting down her pen, Laura knew she had been wrong. Driving that back road, returning to the guest house late at night thinking about her mother, she thought of her new work as an homage to her. Or Gerhard Richter. Mommy/ Gerhard, what a combo. But it was little Peggy, who never got to be Jackie Kennedy and was turning fifty, who was the real hero of the shadow and fog series. She remembered the Big Duck. From the Big Duck in Quogue to Peggy's fiftieth, that was, indeed, a festival of miracles.

Packing up the cottage, stripping the bed, washing the sheets and towels, Laura grinned to herself over the book-end quality of that time. When she finished the series and hopefully had a show at her New York gallery, she'd hire the biggest limo she could to pick up Peggy so she could do her Jackie wave all the way down to Soho and arrive feeling like a star.

Hey, Ma, look; we've outlived you. All of us have. And we're just fine. We've survived both the having and the not having of you — as I pray my daughter survives the having, and at times, the not having me.

So went the tagline of that thought. Laura had nothing to redeem her mother from. No shadow. No fog. No shame. No blame.

We're all just trying to get it right.

Maybe that was the legacy.

CHAPTER 16

Some Nights There's Nothing to do but Paint the Ceiling

LAURA DIDN'T CRY anymore. She hadn't for several years. Well, that wasn't exactly true. When extremely fatigued or under medicated, she could lapse into teenage tears. There were also hormonally induced tears. Other than that, she felt dried up, no fluids coming from any opening in her body, as she herself would say, including pussy juice. She felt on a subliminal level that she had no use for it.

And then there was the happiness gene. She'd decided that she'd been born without it, that its absence had been the source of her problems all those years. Which was a relief. To find out, after years of struggle and blame, that the basis for all her misery was as simple as missing a microscopic chromosome, a DNA malfunction, a genetic loss, a circumstance having nothing to do with her, i.e., not her fault, was a great comfort to her. Oh, phew. There are pills for that, was her first thought. She would have preferred to be lacking the sadness gene, but what the hell. Armed with that new and freeing info, Laura was becoming, if not happy, which, as medical science and her therapist had confirmed was impossible, then at least relaxed. Maybe even edging toward content, though that was a long way off. There were still challenges to address. She needed to be painting. When she went too long without painting, the sediment rose to the surfaces bubbling into sad, stupid thoughts. Thoughts that belonged vibrant or muted on canvas.

She'd had sex with Ben recently and several things about it seemed off. Ben was indeed the love of her life. Not one to use that bullshit expression "soul mate," she knew from the beginning that Ben was her home. That he was the source of anything and everything good that flowed from her heart. Although handsome, she had always loved that tall, lanky, angular face look, it was who he was beneath the sugar coating that got her. Sam had led with kindness. Ben with goodness. His goodness arrived ahead of him so by the time he got there the door was wide open. The thing Laura sensed about Ben when they first started dating was that whatever happened in life, he'd protect her. It was the thing, the one thing she'd always wanted since she was a little girl sitting in the hallway outside of her parents' bedroom listening to her parents scream obscenities at each other. She'd been her mother's protector although it should've been the other way around. Her mother was just too vulnerable for her own good and her father was too much of a drunk for his. Laura wished and prayed for her own savior back then, but no one ever came. Long ago she'd buried her fervent need for someone to see the freckled-face girl burdened by abuse and dysfunction and rescue her. To be her champion. Ben. She knew he would stand by her side, sword in hand, for the rest of her life.

❧

BUT IT was Grace he put on a pedestal. Men could do that: put their firstborn daughters at the top of a golden ladder firmly cemented at the base.

Laura, of course, knew nothing of that in her own childhood. Sitting on a bar stool in an Irish bar in Long Island was her pedestal. Ben would and did give Grace the best of everything. They ain't called princesses for nothing. It started before Grace was even out of the womb. That great love affair. The crib, the baby blankets, even the wallpaper in her nursery had to be "the Best." The jealousy quietly crept in. Laura tried to feel ashamed of it, but all she could feel was a low-grade resentment take root. Her heart over-flowed with love for her baby girl, too, so a part of her loved seeing Grace shining like the morning sun on top of her pedestal. But the green worm, once there, never fully went away.

They had what any onlooker would describe as a won-derful life. The thing about Ben, other than the corner of his heart that was wide open and clean as the day he was born, and of course his undeniable sex appeal, a god-given gift to get girls in trouble for sure, was that he wouldn't ever abandon her. She could love him more, or less, depending on the day. And he'd stay 'til the end. That, of course, made him the man she'd love forever. His eyes were so blue, lighter than cobalt, darker than baby, and honest. But every time she painted him, she never got them right. Hard as she tried. Then there was his smell. Laura, having been taught by a wise woman in that phone booth years earlier, loved the smell of Ben's neck. Inhaling, she'd say, "It's all about your neck, my love," and she'd be off to the races.

"WONDERFUL," THOUGH, was not how she'd been feeling lately. The words to describe how she'd been feeling didn't start with "w" and had no *wow* sounds. They were all *d* words, such as *down, disillusioned, depressed.* Sex had always helped her combat the effects of those *d* words.

But not the other night.

The other night she felt more outside of the event than participatory, watching instead of melting, scents more

foreign than familiar. It felt faintly disturbing. Staring at the
ceiling, she welcomed stray thoughts. After counting the
ninth crack, she decided it was time to paint the ceiling. She
knew not to linger but moved on to the colors she'd use to
paint the ceiling.

CHAPTER 17

Croissant Dreams

"HAVE YOU FORGOTTEN that you are my page for today?" What a beautiful line, thought Laura, digging in her bag for a pen to scribble it down. Someone on NPR was reading Rilke for their annual fund drive. Laura pulled over, killing time before she could drive up to the carpool line without getting yelled at by the carpool cop. Like a lot of people with small jobs who needed to assert themselves, he could be nasty as hell, and took opening the carpool lane at 3:05 P.M., and not a second before, very seriously. "Back of the line. Next time it's carpool court." Pen found; Laura jotted the quote down on the inside cover of her book, then laughed to herself about how weird it would be after she died, when Gracie or Ben or someone would have to go through her things. She had quotes, notes, snippets of poetry, opening sentences, sketches, and drawings stashed all over the place: in hardcovers, paperbacks, notebooks, journals, on parking tickets, and old dry cleaner receipts hidden in handbags on the top shelf in her closet. Sometimes she worried that whoever found those words that she'd seen fit to record, the faces she'd sketched and been moved to keep for further inspection, that he, she, or they might think she led an unhappy life, which wasn't the truth. The truth was not anymore; she had an excellent life, of which the sadness was but a part.

"My page for today." The romance of that struck her mind before it sunk into her heart. Laura closed her eyes and lingered for a moment. Will you be my page for today—just for the day, and I will stay up all night writing about you—stay up, sipping coffee in a café in Paris that never closes, bleary-eyed, yet still writing. They'll bring me more coffee and fresh croissants and I'll go on a little longer.

The sound of a leaf blower, like a dental drill on steroids, startled her and snapped her out of Paris and back to Melrose Avenue, where the SUV parade into Grace's school's driveway was in full swing. Turning on the engine, shifting into gear, it was time to join the parade, leaving another page empty. Perhaps that's what the sadness was about.

CHAPTER 18

Louise Bourgeois Got it Right

LAURA'S SUMMER WAS over. She painted her way through June, through July, and traveled away August. There were places she didn't get enough of and wanted to go back to. There was sleep lost through jet lag that, although lost, was never lethal.

At one point in their travels, at the Centre Pompidou in Paris, Laura sat down on a bench on the third level, looking out at the rooftops, happy to be off her feet, the balls of which were hot and throbbing. Both her daughter and her husband were still out there somewhere in the permanent collection. She was hungry and tired. She wanted to eat dinner that last night in Paris at the rooftop restaurant. It had a deck that opened to the whole city with a spectacular view. Ben had nixed that idea, saying it was too expensive. Having several pairs of stunning Parisian shoes well hidden in her suitcase, which she would later say, "Oh, I've had these for years" if asked, she could live with that. Hot feet and fatigue helped to let that rooftop view be enjoyed by others.

So she sat on the bench thinking about Louise Bourgeois. About Louise's mother series that she'd just seen. How angry it felt to her! And how good it felt to be free from her husband and daughter, if only for a few minutes, and let her mind free float over Paris. She started fantasizing she was in her twenties or thirties and alone, that she had choices and was brave. To be brave and alone in Paris, there was a dream.

Laura could have used a few more days, weeks, possibly months, alone with her husband to find inspiration in him again. Grace had, since day one, commanded if not demanded his attention. Then again, having someone to hand him off to wasn't so bad. Her husband's intensity, that once excited her, exhausted her. It compromised her immune system, of that she was sure. The problem was, she couldn't conceive of loving anyone as much as she loved him. She was tired of sharing him with the pedestal girl. Of how easy it was for him to give to her. If she, Laura, even hinted in that direction, he'd counter with, "We're the grown-ups, we don't need as much." Speak for yourself, Buddy, she yelled from the tunnel of arrested development. Then a sudden urge to march herself into Hermès, smiling a well-pronounced "Bonjour" would come over her. It was high time for Grace, seventeen and a lanky, long-legged beauty reminiscent of her father. It was high time for Grace to give him back.

Laura's mind leapt from Paris to a deli in New York City. She was seventeen again. She hadn't seen her father in months. He'd just returned from a stint in rehab after kissing the floor yet again and being hauled out on a stretcher. He was, in fact, clean, sober, tan, sporting good news and a new attitude. She wasn't buying any of it. She'd agreed to meet him because she needed seventy-five dollars. It was for rent on an apartment over on West Sixty-Ninth Street. She was sharing it with a new friend, a sketchy but beautiful model named Karen from New Jersey. Legs that never stopped, platinum hair down her back and a cherubic face, with a wealthy mother who paid her share of the rent. Laura had written her father at the rehab place in Florida asking for the money. He said he'd give it to her in a week when he got home. He wouldn't just mail it. Too easy. He wanted to meet in person so she could see how good he looked. That was a ship that never sailed, just sunk into the harbor. She moved into the apartment, despite the old man's talk. Although, true to form, he only gave her fifty dollars.

Ben and Gracie suddenly appeared and together addressed her, their words overlapping—"Laura," "Mom"—startling her back into the moment. Paris was so very far from the deli on Eighty-Sixth Street or the apartment on West Sixty-Ninth.

Again, they each called her. Again, their names for her, Laura, and Mom, collided on their way into her ears. Suddenly she wilted. She felt tired and sad. Sad she had never had the chance to be alone and brave in Paris, sad she didn't like her daughter a lot on too many days. Sad that she spent time wondering if she'd ever feel sexually attracted to her husband again, or if her daughter would ever give him back.

Gathering herself to move on with them, she glanced over the Paris rooftops once more. The sky was so blue. Blue and crisp. Such a Paris blue sky. Would she have liked herself at seventeen? No, not at all.

LAURA'S FATHER was many-faceted. As we all are, Laura thought. Only it was her father's many-faceted aspects that shaped her, molded her, tortured, and damaged her. It was the anxiety over which facet she'd wake up to every morning, and which one would walk through the door every night, which she credited for her lifelong need to bite her cuticles until she bled.

Fathers and daughters. A centuries-old dynamic. Baby Cleopatra probably had her old man wrapped around her finger like a stack of gold snake rings back in 69 BC. Laura had put thousands if not hundreds of thousands of dollars into the exploration of the subject, the father-daughter dynamic, and knew there was more onion left to peel. She felt she had forgiven him though. The other day she thought of looking up his birthday—June 18th, or possibly July. Her mother's, December 3rd, she had always known and acknowledged. Since she felt forgiveness (was it that, or just the absence of pain—the numbness of the hardened scab on the wound?), she might acknowledge his birthday. She could bake him a cake from one of the Kitchen Goddess's books and place it on his grave if she knew where it was. She could buy a pint of rye whisky and give it to a homeless guy in his honor. Though why rush things?

The last time Laura saw her dad was that time in the Croydon Deli on Eighty-Sixth Street and Madison Avenue. Once settled at a table for two in full view, he announced that he'd bought a house in Long Island and would be moving out of the two-bedroom on Park in a few weeks with her younger sister and Crazy Kate the maid. "Starting over," he said, like she'd believe him.

"I'm sober as a judge," he told her repeatedly during their meal at the Croydon. He looked good. He'd put on weight. She didn't know why he'd gone to Florida to dry out that time, instead of his time-honored Silver Hill in Connecticut. Fun in the sun? Florida seemed to have suited him. Tall and trim. When on a bender, he resembled Ichabod Crane. With the weight, a tan, his white hair combed straight back, and wearing a sports jacket, the old man looked damn good. Handsome. She saw a glimpse of the young man her mother fell in love with.

Smiling his sober smile, he told Laura the house on the island was in Woodmere near the beach club. He asked her to move back with him, "Come back home" was how he phrased it. She had left home six months earlier after their last big blowout when he was "three sheets to the wind," as her mother used to call it, and, on a tear about something, he slapped her in the face. "If you hit me one more time," Laura said, "I'm outta here." *Bam,* he did, and she was. She had spent a few nights at a friend's house and then answered an ad in the *New York Times* classified, a part-time babysitting job with room and board listed by a single mother up on 102nd and Fifth Avenue. The room was good. The kid, a six-year-old girl, not so good. Workable, though, and it was peaceful.

Sitting with her father at a table for two in full view of the deli's baked goods, Laura faced glazed cherries, row upon neatly stacked row of sugar cookies, and chocolate cakes that stood at least a foot and a half high. As her father spoke, Laura, determined not to get sucked in, was more interested in getting cash out of his pocket than the *blah blah blah* promises made to be broken. Shifting her gaze from her father's sincere, well-shaven face to the chocolate cakes and back again, she had to admit, handsome and sober was a winning combo. He'd sold his seat on the New York Stock Exchange for a record price according to the *Wall Street Journal.* More than a quarter of a million, as they said back in 1968 when a million meant enough that even a quarter of it was noted.

The plan was to have his whole family back under one roof. Lucy, who was away at college, would come home and talk to him again. A new start for all of them.

"I'll think about it" was all Laura could say, sipping her Tab. Spooning cottage cheese onto a saltine, evening it off to form a neat layer covering the whole cracker, she had stopped listening. She didn't want to hear any more about how it was going to be. Every word he said just made her surer and surer of one thing. That she wanted a piece of chocolate cake. With an ice-cold glass of milk instead of the tin-tasting Tab, the way she'd have had it when her mother was alive.

Back in Paris, on the third floor of the Pompidou, they continued to overlap her name, "Mom/Laura," earth to mom, but mom was still at the Croydon finishing her chocolate cake.

CHAPTER 19

Becoming Him

H E WON'T GO away because fathers never go away. If you've never had one, then it's even worse—the dream of him never goes away. It stays forever and, in many cases, ruins your life. Laura was in her early fifties when she realized that. She thought she'd be further along with her life. Secure. She thought she would've shed all that childhood insecurity, but it was back with a fucking vengeance. Fathers may die but they don't go away. Ben had started to remind her of her father. He was "watching every penny," and never silently, spilling his innate insecurity like birdseed all over her well-being. She resented it. He was never like that before.

Laura never thought of Ben as being anything like her father. But with age, his own fears began to manifest in ways similar to her father's. It felt like ice hitting the exposed tooth that needs a root canal. She couldn't take it unmedicated.

Now, every time they got home from a vacation, the moment they'd walk in the door, Ben would drop his bags and go straight into his office, grabbing his letter opener as he hit the chair. Just couldn't resist the siren song of those bills. By the time she got into bed, he'd be singing his "now we've got to save" song, flushing whatever joy the vacation had given her right down the toilet. She wanted to claw him for that. That and other things she couldn't stand anymore, real or imagined, glared at her like the oozing sores of her childhood.

The truth was, she herself had begun to channel her father. She'd begun to use pot the way her father used whiskey. That truth didn't make her happy. The day she drove up to the valet at the Beverly Wilshire Hotel, gave the suited-up boy with the slicked-back ponytail the keys to her car and a ten-dollar bill, and told him she'd be back in five minutes, she saw it. Walking into the lobby quickly glancing in the floor-to-ceiling gold-framed mirror, her father looked back at her.

She'd had ten minutes to get in and out so she could get to school on time for Grace's play without walking in when the lights were out, tripping over everyone, and thereby causing a commotion. She needed to be in her seat, preferably in the middle of the first few rows, so Grace could see her smiling face, beaming love at her. That's what her daughter needed to say her lines correctly.

She'd walked fast, the way she did everything fast, to the reception desk of the hotel and asked for Mrs. Walsh's room please. Mrs. Walsh was the name Veronica, her pot dealer/hooker, who was on a job at the hotel that day, had asked her to use. She called up to Mrs. Walsh in 503. Be right there, Veronica said, and she was. Laura smiled and handed her a book with a fifty-dollar bill tucked inside and Veronica, in her navy Armani suit, looking more like a lady who lunched and less like a hooker about to start a party, handed Laura a Jo Malone gift bag holding a small bar of lime-basil soap and an ounce of pot. Laura was back in her car in nine minutes, tipping the guy another two bucks. At that rate, she'd have time to pull over to her favorite spot and have a puff and still be on time. She raced across town almost euphoric with the sense of security and well-being a full stash brought her. An uncalled-for thought flew in,

interrupting her euphoria. Not a welcome thought but a
ruin-her-party thought: She knew how her father felt the
moment he wrapped his hand around a brown paper bag,
gripping the glass neck of a pint of Scotch.

Well, she thought later that day in her pot-infused
wisdom, one way to forgive them was to become them. And
perhaps there was a lesson to be learned from Ben and his
fucking save money song. Security, isn't that the dream we
all share?

CHAPTER 20

South Pacific

WOULD SEEING THE obvious mean admitting defeat, Laura wondered? Monica, her therapist asked her to "pay attention—look closer—see the obvious—whatever obvious means to you." Monica had suggested that last Thursday at the end of Laura's session. Since then, Laura tried. Good at therapy homework, because at that point she was ready, was past ready, to get on with her life in peace. If therapy assignments were given, Laura did them wholeheartedly. Laziness was not going to be what prevented her from a little peace. What felt obvious was that she needed to let go of the idea of being the perfect mother or rather what a perfect mother did. That fantasy had sabotaged her. It had, in fact, brought about, well, not the *exact* opposite, which would be going too far, but an opposite that at the very least had impeded on the fruition of her desire.

Lately she'd realized that she and Ben didn't have a shared dream anymore. The house, the baby, the yellow lab that loved the baby. Done. Achieved. It wasn't good, everything being vague and up in the air. She couldn't tell if she was floating or sinking. Laura believed in goals, dreams she could visualize and work toward. That's how life had always worked for her.

When she was a young painter living in New York City, divorced from the bad boy with heinous teeth at twenty-five,

she'd had a dream of moving to LA. Every night before falling asleep, she saw LA in her mind, saw Malibu (who knew
it would look like the Jersey Shore), saw herself feeling free
and unencumbered walking down Hollywood Boulevard
(another grave disappointment littered with red-lipped per-
oxide blondes, way past their expiration dates). Lying on
her bed, looking out the window, which Laura did often
when not at CBGB's or Max's, she visualized walking the
beach like Tuesday Weld in *Play It as It Lays*. The picture
became her private goal. When Sam, painter/boyfriend/
lover of surfer chicks, said he was moving to LA, she almost
said, "Of course we are."

Laura knew she was in trouble. She and Ben had vague
goals for the future, their future. Vague was not good.
Vague brought in anything. Vague allowed for mistakes and
messiness.

Laura was not in the mood for mistakes and messiness.
They needed a goal together. Her fear was that their sepa-
rate goals, or their ill-formed, half-defined goals, would mire
them, slow them to a crawl, and make their life together a
joyless event however it shaped out.

She needed to figure out how to be, those days. She
wanted her therapist to tell her how to interact with her
husband. What she really wanted was to lie on the floor and
say, "Tell me, is it me or him, or are the bogeymen trapped
in the tunnel getting free? Give me a goal to save us?"

Driving out of her driveway that morning, she started
singing, "If you don't have a dream, then how ya gonna
have a dream come true?" She heard the original, singsong
show tune in her head as she sang it to herself. Show tunes?
When did her life devolve into show tunes? Heading down
the road, she tried to remember what show it was from but
couldn't. That not being the point, she just continued to
sing.

CHAPTER 21

Oh, That Little Prada Bag

"SEIZED BY OUR own misfortune." Laura couldn't remember if that was a line from a poem or a short story she'd read in the *New Yorker*. Wherever the hell it had come from didn't matter. It was a concept lodged somewhere in her frontal lobe, circling, making its presence known daily. "Seized" is such a harsh word, Laura thought. *Stuck* is better and more to the point. *Stuck* is calmer, gentler, by far, than *seized*. *Stuck* says that one can start up again. *Seized*. *Seized* can suggest violence, murder. Laura sure as hell had no intention of being murdered by her misfortune.

Miss-fortune. Another loaded word formed by two emotionally loaded words on their own. So many ways to take it, Laura thought, pulling into her driveway, relieved yet again to be off the road and behind her gates, knowing Ben and Gracie wouldn't be home for another hour, hour and a half, if she was lucky. Ben picked up Grace from piano at five and they usually stopped for frozen yogurt on the way home to wait out the traffic.

She turned the engine off, keeping the Elvis Costello CD on, and reached into the glove compartment for her black leather makeup bag stuffed behind the car manual. Prada "stash bag," as her friend Stacy called it. She took out her small silver box of weed and the delicate glass pipe, followed by the yellow Bic lighter, prepping for her pre-home-entry ritual. Sitting back, she lit up.

There's the misfortune all humans suffer at some or many points in their lives. Or it could be missing the fortune one had hoped for. Like living a healthy life and being able to watch your children grow up, get married, have children of their own. That was her mother's missed fortune.

Elvis was singing, "Alison, I know this world is killing you," as Laura thought back an hour. She was sitting in her doctor's office playing with the blue heart-shaped paper-weight on his desk.

She let it roll from one hand back to the other while her doctor read her the report from his buddy at Johns Hopkins, confirming his diagnosis that she had Parkinson's.

Elvis crooned in Dolby sound, "I see you've got a hus-band now . . ."

"Yes, I do, Elvis, and a damn cute kid too!" Laura said right back at him.

As she sat parked in her driveway, singing along about Alison and her life, she had the thought that her misfortune might indeed be to emulate her mother's life.

CHAPTER 22

Spooning with Wayne

Her FAMILY ALWAYS accused her of loving her dog more than she loved them. True to her fashion, Laura lied. She told them she could never love her dog, their family dog—which was really hers because she was the only one who had ever taken care of him, despite the promises and protests—more than she loved them. But in a way she did. Not really. But he was easier to love. Her dog, Wayne, half Jack Russell, half Beagle, had more loyalty in his little paws than any human being she'd ever met. But the thing that kept him leagues above anyone was that he was so uncomplicated, and that brought her joy.

She adopted Wayne from the Westside Animal Shelter eight years earlier when their family lab was on her way out, and Grace said she couldn't bear the thought of her dying. Wayne was not the dog she had gone looking for. Thinking another lab, a young one full of life and all that tail-wagging, face-licking energy labs possess, would be good for both Grace and their dying lab. But it was that funny, big-eyed mixed breed who caught her eye and held it. Walter, as he was named by the volunteer at the shelter, literally stopped her in her tracks. Living in the hills as they did, where coyotes still bred, roamed, and foraged for food, cats and small dogs were never safe. Adopting a small to midsize dog wasn't the best idea. But that guy, looking at her with his saucer-size brown eyes, holding her gaze like he'd known her forever, said pick me and she did.

Grace asked, "Mom, are you sick or something? Every time I've asked for a small dog you've said no. 'No, small dogs in the hills are coyote food.' What's up with you now? Besides, Mom, there's a chocolate lab in the next aisle."

"I know, I know," Laura answered, "but there's something about this little cutie. We'd have to be careful and keep him inside at night, just put him on a leash and walk him around before bedtime . . . I don't know . . . this little guy seems to be the one." Laura called him "the one," without her usual deference to her child's desires or even the usual family discussion concerning household pets and vacations. She ran a democracy. Bullshit, she bowed to everyone else's wishes, but that time was different. Grace continued to comment, but Laura didn't listen. She asked the volunteer to open the cage, a urine-stained, cement-block cell dotted with small brown balls of the day's poop. She knelt to catch him and out the little guy jumped, right into her arms.

Grace, immediately jealous of the scene, got into the act, crying, "Let me have him, let me have him!" Changing her tune completely.

By the time they signed the papers, paid the fee, and promised to have him neutered, Grace had renamed Walter "Wayne" and promised to love him forever. But he was Laura's dog. She knew it, and Wayne knew it too.

It was Wayne she told when she was diagnosed with Parkinson's. He was the first to know. He knew it before she told him. Not that it was PD, though he could have known that too. There was a report on NPR about a dog in Scotland who sniffed out people with Parkinson's. Whatever Wayne knew, it was that there was something shitty going on inside of her. He had stopped leaving her alone and insisted on sleeping on the floor on her side of the bed, abandoning the doggie bed he'd slept on for years.

Then he stopped his morning rounds around the pool and garden, preferring to sit by her feet in the kitchen. That went on for a year or so, until the day she came home and looked into his brown eyes, her blue ones tearing up, and said, "You're right, my boy, I'm a mess; I need you," and they climbed into her bed and spooned like lovers.

CHAPTER 23

Her Red Devil Heels

THE SILENT HEART is screaming. The screams would be heard from here to China if the heart could be heard. Thankfully, though, the heart, as stated, is silent. Thankfully for who? Or is it whom?

Laura could never remember that grammatical rule. She was a painter not a writer.

At times Laura felt the need to go into silence. To stop talking completely. To be the listener, the listener of life. To do away with even the slightest need to say a word. There had been days when she'd driven out of her driveway praying her vocal cords would freeze forever. Forced to be mute. No speaking up, no speaking out—no speaking, period. If she couldn't speak, she couldn't argue. Couldn't fight, couldn't say things she'd regret. All she'd be able to do was listen.

Funny how people go to lectures, events, evenings to hear who's speaking, Laura mused. Who spoke? What was said? How about who listened—or what was not said? Laura used to want to be heard. *Listen to me, listen to my idea. Listen to find out who I really am. Listen to me, and like me.*

She found she was caring less about being heard and more about being quiet. As much as she loved, admired, and always found a place for words, they interested her less. They seemed more and more just a waste of breath. Could one go from the talker, the doer, to being the silent observer? She was ready to find out.

Her mother had stopped talking at the end. She had a notebook and a pen dangling from a chain that had hung around her neck like a necklace, and whatever she *had* to say she scribbled on the notepad. That is, until her hand could no long hold the pen. Then she truly was done with words.

The cycles of life amused Laura. *We were babies, uttering our first words, which got chronicled and announced to family members far and wide. We spent our formative years learning words, their meaning, their power—their usage as weapons of mass creation or mass destruction. We grew into teenagers who shouted to be heard, struggled to be listened to. As adults, we were counted on to say things that were smart and meaningful. Whatever words we used, we sought to be effective; we sought to be appreciated. Always, always seeking to be heard. Some of us have had to struggle our whole lives to be heard.*

Maybe the time had come to say nothing at all, Laura thought, driving down the road, away from her house, where too much had been said. From there on out, she would not say another word, just write, like her mother did, until she, too, could no longer hold a pen.

The last line of a poem stuck in her head. It looped 'round and 'round her brain at odd hours, interfering with other thoughts. It was annoying because, just when she thought she was into the swing of things again, meaning feeling upbeat and somewhat excited about life, as rare as those times seemed, the loop started to play, a maudlin powder keg threatening to explode.

"Caught partway between love and death," was the line circling Laura's brain. *Partway between love and death—playing on an old wooden seesaw. Love straddles one end; death's fat ass, the other.*

Laura talked to Lloyd; he had left about five messages. Each sounded a little more urgent than the last, so she finally decided to talk to him. Lloyd, her ex-art dealer, a short bespectacled man who carried no excess flesh on his body, was always meticulously dressed in custom-made suits. His shirts were either blue or white without a crease in sight. He was the only man she knew who wore gold, monogrammed cufflinks. They hadn't spoken in three years. Since she no longer painted, there was nothing to speak about.

After the *hellos* and *how are you doings* and *miss you darling*, Lloyd got right to it. He had a call from someone interested in buying one of her paintings. Something worth speaking about.

"Wow! Which one?" was her surprised response. She hadn't exhibited in years, three and five months, to be precise, but who was counting. She had put her brushes down never to be picked up again. Let's be clear, even though she was at the top of her game, the art world didn't shed a big round tear. No, at her height she was at best semi-known.

"So, who called and why?" she queried.

A man who went to her last show at Lloyd's Gallery. His wife was a fan, and there was a piece she loved, but at the time he wasn't buying. The piece, part of her cloud series of thickly layered oil on medium canvases, had sold for $7,000. She was pleased as well as shocked that the show had sold out. Quit while you're ahead was her plan all along, she could have said. Toss and splat was never her style.

Apparently the man was upset upon hearing she'd stopped painting. Wanted Lloyd to find out if whoever had bought that painting wanted to sell. He'd pay more than the asking price from three years ago. His wife had cancer. He wanted to cheer her up, fill her last days, months, years if she were lucky, with things, beautiful things to make her happy.

Well, didn't that jus' hit home. Her cynical devil woke up and raised its ugly head. *Why, oh, why the fuck did they always wait until death came knocking before they're willing to spare no expense to make us happy?*

That little devil, still such a part of her, was out running around, kicking up her red devil heels. For years, years, she'd begged Ben to move to Santa Barbara. First, she used Grace. The schools were better. Then the land value, getting more bang for the buck. Always a big appeal. Many times she tried the truth; her dream was to live at the beach, away from the hustle, bustle, and shitty traffic of LA. For years, he'd said no. Pulling every excuse out of every pocket to mask the true reason he couldn't allow the thought—her thought, her wish, her dream—of moving to become more than a thought. He already had his dream.

She remembered exactly where she was—in the car, of course—stuck in traffic on Sunset, conscious of the two pints of Haagen-Dazs and four sticks of Irish butter in the grocery bag on the back seat melting because the air-conditioning was on the fritz, when the sentence formed in her head: I'd have to be dying for him to move us to Santa Barbara. Little did she know that having Parkinson's would be good enough.

"Did you check who bought the painting the guy wants?" she asked, not sure if Lloyd was still on the line or if the call had dropped. The cell service in their area of Santa Barbara was iffy.

"I did," he said, assuring the connection.

"Your sister-in-law, Dinah."

Laura thought, knowing Ben's sister, she would be thrilled to sell it and make a profit.

"Call him and tell him you think you can get it for him. Add several thousand. Take your fee; pay Dinah 10 percent over what she paid, and what's left donate to stem cell research. Oh, and I'd like to write a personal note to the wife." The red devil had already begun to write; "Pitiful, isn't it, they wait until we're dying to say that coveted sentence, 'Yes, my darling, if that would make you happy.'"

CHAPTER 24

Replacement Shopping

LAURA DIDN'T SEE widows on her doorstep. She saw replacements. She sought out replacements. At the market, at Starbucks, at dinner parties. Years earlier she would have cast an evil eye on those women, blondes mostly, and high achievers. She began to search for them wearing her brightest smile. She wouldn't be the one wearing the black outfit. It's a fucking shame, she laughed to herself, her black Irish humor her biggest asset, as being a rich widow would have been fun.

Ben had been a "good Jewish husband" and provided nicely for her, thinking being ten years her senior and coming from a line of men whose lousy hearts gave out by age sixty-two, he would be exiting before her. Good thinking, except for Ben and everything about him, including his organs, Laura was sure of that, came from his maternal rather than his paternal side. Since that was the case, he'd be living well into his nineties. Laura had stopped fantasizing about the vintage 280 Mercedes sport coupe she'd always wanted.

When she was younger and didn't know better, she'd lick her wounds after a big fight with such trivial thoughts. After a particularly nasty blowout, usually about money or sometimes about Grace. If it had been off the charts bad, she'd curl up and think of the ten thousand ways she'd get back at that person she'd married while rocking herself to sleep. Like counting sheep, she'd count the zillions she'd spend on the frivolous things he would find most offensive.

She'd have such fun with those fantasies! And she was so good at them! She could almost feel the weight of the shopping bags filled with shoes, not a markdown among them, in every color, as she carried them out to the car of her dreams. They gave her pleasure and relief.

With her Parkinson's getting worse and Ben getting A-plus checkups, the binge shopping and the sport coupe were over, and she was eying blondes at the supermarket. Someone kind. Someone who had her own money, would be a plus. Someone used to caring for others was a must. She loved her Ben with her whole heart and wanted him well cared for.

It wasn't as enjoyable, though, as replacement fantasizing, as the 280 SL, top down, overflowing with Neiman's shopping bags racing down Rodeo Drive.

CHAPTER 25

All's Lost Shit

HER MOTHER'S BED always felt warm. Lived in and warm, if not safe. Safety wasn't found on those sheets, littered with books, magazines, newspapers, and tissues, her dog, Bosco, resting at the foot, and her mother's pink, quilted bed jacket somewhere in the mix, but love was.

Laura's mother was a woman whose body always felt like ice, but her bed was always welcoming, inviting, and where Laura wanted to be. To be protective of a woman so fragile her own blood couldn't keep her warm. She'd been thinking about her mother a lot lately. More than usual and feeling her presence; not in an eerie way, just in a "oh, there you are" way.

She was in the waiting room, starting to resent how long she'd been waiting. Jesus, the least they could do would be to upgrade the damn magazines. Who the hell is going to read *Woman's Day* was the thought she'd had before slipping into thinking about her mother's bed. For some reason, she couldn't remember the trigger to that thought. She used to let it bother her, when her thoughts, her to-do thoughts or her what-to-do-next thoughts silently fluttered away like butterflies disappearing in a garden.

Waiting. It was the waiting she hated. Waiting in those rooms that had all begun to look alike, with their modern art reproductions and pastel paint jobs and faux leather couches. Same mahogany wing chairs and crappy magazines. Beverly Hills, Santa Barbara, if she went to a doctor somewhere in Wisconsin, the waiting room would look the same. Her Parkinson's had progressed, according to her latest report. She was waiting to have the second opinion confirmed and assessed by "the specialist," the head honcho himself that both opinion number one and number two had advised her to see. Although Laura had little faith in number one anymore. She thought he was a drug addict, opinion number one. Pills. Laura ran into him once on an art walk in Venice. They had coffee at a café, and all he wanted to talk about was some well-known and highly revered surgeon in Chicago who had managed to hide his heroin habit for his entire career.

Laura's mother never had MS, like her doctor first diagnosed. Those years in bed, those days, months, and years her mother spent living in the king-size bed she shared with Laura's father in the house in Sands Point, those years it was never MS. Her mother was just paralyzed from a broken heart no amount of gin could fix, no matter how much she tried.

When her mother finally got the correct diagnosis of ALS, it was a short hop, skip, and jump to Never-Never Land. ALS. All's Lost Shit.

Ironic in the off-center way that Laura's mind worked, how her mother froze on her way to the grave. She'd be shaking all the way to hers.

CHAPTER 26

It's All About a Proper Goodbye

HER HUSBAND HAD gone south, as of late, in ways that weren't pleasing to her. He worried. He always worried, but he was worrying more, and it worried her. She felt his worrying exacerbated her PD.

She decided to talk to Grace about the Parkinson's before Ben the Worrywart spilled the beans. She also thought, wrongly, she could use a confidant, felt like she needed one, and it wasn't Ben. Gentle Ben . . . was that a movie or a song, both? Oh shit, she remembered, it may have been a Michael Jackson song about a rat! A deer, her Ben, never a rat if one were playing the what-animal-would-you-be game. But she wasn't in the mood for games. And Grace being her confidant? One toke over the mother/daughter line.

She was in the mood for a plan. It was time, and, aside from her beloved Wayne, she trusted her daughter more than anyone else in the world. Funny how Gracie was the one who knew her best, Laura thought. She felt like her daughter had studied her from the day she was born, never missing a move. Not a trick. Not a joint smoked behind the oak tree outside of the kitchen. Not a shopping bag stashed in the trunk of her car for days until it was safe to bring it in without prying eyes. Glued to her side for all her formative years, Gracie witnessed it all.

If her mother had told Laura and her sisters the truth, how would it have been? If instead of saying she'd had a stroke and was getting better—while Laura saw her go from cane to walker to wheelchair—she had said, straight out: "I have ALS, and I'm going to get worse and then I'm going to die, so let's discuss it." What if she had sat down with Laura, her father, and Lucy—Peggy being way too young—and said, "It's not pretty, but we can do this together and help prepare each other. We can do that while praying they come up with a cure . . ." Would that have been better, made it easier, changed the outcome? Did her mother really pray for a cure, or was she grateful for a way out?

Laura believed it would have mattered, made a difference, but who really knew? She did know what fucked her up the most all those years was not getting to say goodbye to her mother. To go through whatever words, touches, and tears there needed to be for her to move on into life without her. The big goodbye that would allow her to have any sense of peace, never happened.

They had been in their mother's room in the hospital, she, Lucy, and Peggy, having just been summoned from school. Her mother, with her head on the pillow, looked smaller, more delicate than she had when Laura had left for school that morning. Pale, her mother looked like the sheet she rested on. Bony too. Laura could see her mother's hands on top of the white sheet and noted her white wrist bones sticking out. Lotta white going on in that room. Walls, nurses' uniforms, bones.

Laura's father and uncles were in the room, lining the walls, wearing their workday suits and tragic faces. When the priest arrived, Laura and her sisters were ushered out. Her aunt Laura said they would come back later. They needed to eat something, and their mother needed to have a nap.

Eat? Laura had thought at the time, who the fuck could
eat. She put up a fight to stay, telling them she'd wait outside her mother's room and get something from the vending machine if she got hungry. But it was a no go. Her aunt
dragged them home.

Never to see their mother alive again.

Next glance was after the main man at Campbell's
Funeral Home had waved her hair and put the wrong shade
of red on her lips.

It was all in the saying goodbye that could free you or
freeze you, Laura thought. In her heart, she felt she was
preparing to say goodbye to Ben on some level. Confus-
ing, because she felt she might still have a choice. Leave the
party sooner, with Ben finding someone young and cash-
rich to walk him into old age—or fight to stay in the game?

Fight the good fight. Fight hard.

She was Irish, after all.

She'd talk to Grace. It was time. She wouldn't lean on
her or lie to her. But she would appropriately omit.

CHAPTER 27

Mirror, Mirror on the Wall

"FUCK," SHE SCREAMED, and Grace came running.

"What's the fuck about, Ma? You OK?" Gracie tripped over herself trying to get to her. To stop whatever bad was happening to her. But nothing bad had happened to Laura. She'd just looked in the mirror. The shock of it sent her reeling.

"Oh, my God," Laura said aloud, that time lower and with less drama, aka anger, than before.

When the hell did that happen, or had she been in such denial she just couldn't see?

Obviously, she answered herself.

Obviously she'd been wearing blinders for months.

Staring into the mirror that morning, she saw someone staring back at her who scared the shit out of her. Who was that? Whose face? Whose eyes, whose nose, whose lips, so thin and lined? Vertical grooves aligned like soldiers between her upper lip and her nostrils. One could hide coins in those grooves.

"Mom, calm down," said the good daughter. "Mom, you're being silly. You're having a bad morning."

"No, my love," Laura said. "Fuck how I feel . . . it's about how I look. I'm sixty and look ninety."

They were in her bathroom. The light on the magnifying mirror was on, as well as the overhead light, and the window shade was up. Way too much light on the sad subject.

"Mom, you look the same as always."

"Saying that only makes it worse. Could you pull the shade down, honey?" Laura said to her daughter, who was sitting on the covered toilet seat, her tanned legs that stretched for days dangling over the side of the tub. At twenty-five, Grace was in a word, *gorgeous*. *Flawless* worked too. Tall, lean, and lanky, with a full mane of black hair. Even in her current position she looked like a full-grown woman. She looked like Ben. His coloring, his height. Laura always joked that Ben wore the dominant genes in the family.

Working for a start-up in San Francisco allowed Grace to go home more often, which she'd taken to doing. At some point, maybe it was in her third year of college, Grace had morphed from the selfish teenager who bucked Laura at every turn, into a caring young woman her mother couldn't get enough of.

"No worries, darling," Laura said, regaining her composure. "I'm fine. Just didn't sleep well and I don't know what happened when I looked in the mirror. Just lost it." Lost it, she thought. Found the ugly truth is more like it.

Over the previous six months, her hair had fallen out like it was shedding season. Her skin, tending to be dry normally, had withered like a leaf in the fall, drying, shriveling up, and cracking. And her eyes? The window to her soul, as well as one of her best features (one boyfriend years ago nicknamed them "headlights"), had become dull, lusterless. Please get thee a window washer, they pleaded with her, if you ever wanna glimpse of that soul again.

Medical science. Ya gotta love it. It can cure you by killing the you you've always known. Her latest med had taken its toll, and then some.

"It's okay, baby," Laura said. "Like I said, I had a bad
night. I kept waking up, trying to remember my dream and
then not being able to get back to sleep. I'm just tired. I
looked in the mirror, which is always a bad, bad thing to do
straight out of bed. Won't be doing that again."

Of course, she knew what had happened. She saw herself. Saw who she had become. Gone was the full face with
cheekbones that pointed toward her temples. Where was
the spray of freckles that fanned out across her nose, giving
her that look of eternal youth? Did they fade, fall off? Did
her latest medicine eat them? And those jowls? Why hadn't
she seen them before?

Smiling at Grace, she pulled the curtain down on the
play. Stage closed. Show over. Mom's fine. Her daughter,
busy filing her toenails over the tub with the nail file she
grabbed from the bathroom counter, wasn't upset by her
appearance. Obviously that meant that she, Laura, had
looked that bad for a while.

But what did she expect? To have a disease that made
her head bop and her feet freeze, and still look cute? She had
never quite achieved pretty, but cute she was sure of and
she had made it work for her. With her shapely figure and
long straight blonde hair and that spray of freckles across
her nose, she could work any room with confidence. That
was the package that had gotten her that far. Yes, that far,
she thought to herself. And how far was that, exactly? Looking at her daughter, working the life off that emery board,
Laura thought, *It's your turn now, baby. Mine has passed. It's
yours now, girl. Go. Give it all you've got.* She started to laugh.
Grace looked up, swinging her leg off the tub.

"What now, Mom? First it was, fuck, like you'd found
a rat in your shoe and now you're laughing? You're scaring
me, Ma." Grace liked calling her "Ma," like they were hillbillies or from Queens. It was their thing. Laura signed all
her emails to Grace, "Ma."

"Nothing, honey, I just thought about something funny."

She didn't tell her daughter that what struck her as funny at that moment was that a week earlier, she had decided that maybe what she needed was to have an affair. That with Grace living her life and Ben doing Ben, a good old-fashioned affair, a hard dick with no strings and a personality that could make her laugh till she peed, was what she needed. Forget the trial meds, the vitamin drips, forget the acupuncture . . . a nice dick and a few good laughs was the prescription Dr. Laura had written for herself less than a week earlier. Fantasy Island. Again, always a good go-to place.

"Ha," Laura blurted, glancing back at the mirror, "not with this face, baby!"

"What did you say, Ma?"

"Your face, baby. Just saying how much I love your face."

CHAPTER 28

Choke on That Meatball

SHE WAS TOO damn tired those days to do the good girl/ good wife dance anymore. Her mother had come to her in a dream one night and told her she would be seeing her soon. When Laura awoke from the dream, she felt happy and exhilarated, but then she remembered it was just a dream. The next night she dreamed she was turning one hundred and when she woke, she felt miserable.

Living until one hundred wasn't a wish she'd ever had, and she really couldn't say for sure that she even wanted to stick around until seventy. She couldn't tell that to a soul. No one would really understand except for her mother and talking to her was like talking to Jesus. It was a conversation that only took place in the head, maybe the heart, but certainly not sitting in the kitchen over a cup of coffee. She'd known all along it was the disappointment that killed her mother, not whatever disease they called it. It was the heartbreak of finding out that her husband, decorated marine, blue-eyed charmer, Mr. Personality, couldn't rise to the occasion, any occasion, without a drink.

That while she, her mother, was looking for a hero, he, her father, was looking for a mother.

Aren't they all?

Laura's symptoms were becoming more pronounced. She and Ben were at a concert one night and her head had started shaking like a dashboard doll in a car heading downhill at high speed. The couple next to them got up and moved, they were so unnerved.

There was nothing she could say or do. She could only sit there and breathe through the shaking. She'd learned that getting upset only prolonged it, so she stayed put, uttering her latest inner mantra. *I don't give a flying fuck.*

On the way home, Ben started babbling about going to see her doctor with her to ask him about some new trial he'd heard about. Ben thought he saw it on *60 Minutes* and said he would research it.

You do that, Ben.

Kind, caring, mothering, and smothering. Laura's bitchy attitude had nothing to do with him. She went deaf in the car, thought about her mother, and flashed back to Sands Point.

The Italian restaurant in the village. Cassalaro's. It was their family's Friday night go-to unless her mother was frying scallops in butter at home. But her mother had stopped frying anything by that time. The whole family was eating at Cassalaro's, which was an oddity. Usually it was just takeout. Ziti with marinara and pizza. But there they were, sitting, eating, laughing . . . laughing like Mr. and Mrs. Good Parents and their three swell kids. Laura's father was on the wagon and her mother was drinking ginger ale. Laura was very clear on the memory and remembered the green bottle of Canada Dry in front of her mother "like it was yesterday," to borrow the tried and true.

It was a good night. Until they got up to leave.

Every table was full. Laura saw faces she knew from school. Mrs. Cittadino, the crossing guard on her block, was there with her husband. No kids. Mrs. Cittadino, usually dressed in her olive-drab crossing-guard uniform with the yellow sash, wore a red dress with ample cleavage. Date night.

When they got up to leave, Laura's mother's right leg gave out. Wouldn't move forward. Buckled beneath her. She fell back in her chair, so everyone sat down in unison and waited for her to try again. Flushing, blushing, Laura and her two sisters turned their own shade of shame. Heads were turning. They waited. Laura felt trickles of sweat dribbling down her armpits as her mother got up to give it another go. She got the leg moving. Not in sync with the left one, but moving, nonetheless. The parade to the front door could have taken five minutes but felt like an hour, eyes escorting them past the red-and-white tablecloths the whole time.

An hour doing the walk of shame out of a goddamn pizza parlor.

Fuck you. Eat your food, eleven-year-old Laura wanted to scream at the lookie-loos staring at her mother like she was a sideshow freak.

Fuck you. Choke on that meatball, she wanted to say to all the faces, all the eyes.

The whispering mouths, "She's drunk." "And in front of her children."

Driving home the image of her mother's face, stoic yet so sad, wouldn't leave her.

She pressed the button to open the sunroof of the car. Hot and claustrophobic, she needed to look at the moon and the stars.

She needed to lose herself in the sky.

"I'm the one walking out of Cassalaro's now, Mom."

CHAPTER 29

She Didn't Really Want Tuna on Rye

WHAT IS THE line about sorrow? Some hidden sorrow, some unnamed sorrow? Some random sorrow? Who the hell knew, thought Laura, tired of trying to remember the exact line. It was the word that grabbed her, so the rest was just words. *Sorrow* glommed onto her and stuck to her the way it always had. *Sorrow* is my homing pigeon, she thought, always flying back to me, never ever losing its way.

She was sitting in her doctor's waiting room yet again. Third time that month. Ratcheting up those visits as new symptoms appeared each week. Marlena, her housekeeper, who had recently added driver to her résumé, was sitting next to her, reading a three-year-old *People* magazine. At first Laura felt uncomfortable about Marlena accompanying her to her appointments, but, like everything else, she'd gotten used to it.

"Marlena, could you see if there's an *Architectural Digest* over there," Laura would say. Pointing toward the stack of magazines at the far side of the room was a hell of a lot easier than having to get up and shake her way over to the stack herself.

Laura's shaking had increased in the previous two months to where it was almost comical. She used the word *comical* just in case there was any chance of fooling herself into seeing anything, anything at all amusing about it. But it wasn't comical, amusing, or funny in the least. It was gross. Disgusting and highly disturbing. And sad. Laura's way of coping was to make fun of it, make fun of herself before anyone else had a chance to.

"Be careful, Ben, or I'll bring you a cup of coffee."

He was annoying her over some random thing she couldn't even remember, something small and inconsequential that didn't even bear mentioning, the way he did those days, and she asked him to please change the conversation.

"What's wrong with my conversation?" he asked, using that wounded little-boy tone that only made it worse for her.

It's boring, Ben. Your conversation is all about my health and it's boring and tiresome, and I am sick of it. Oh, to just let that fly straight from her mouth with all the force she usually used to hold it down. *But that would be cruel. And there would be no turning back. No whooshing it all in, sucking it back in one big breath.*

She couldn't be cruel. As much as she would have loved to at times, Laura knew that even in her state, which was a goddamn mess, he was much more fragile than she'd ever be. She knew he was just trying to show his concern. The most important thing she knew was that the real source of her annoyance wasn't Ben. He was just the fall guy.

"Marlena, I've an idea. You walk over to the diner and order us sandwiches to take home. I'll have a tuna on rye and get whatever you want, OK?" She handed her housekeeper, who was chomping at the bit to get away from the waiting room full of shaking heads and hands, a fifty-dollar bill and sent her on her way.

Laura wanted a tuna sandwich the way her dog wanted fleas, but she couldn't think of another way to ditch her sweet companion. She absolutely didn't want Marlena going into the exam room with her, adding to the carnival

of humiliation. Having discarded the *Architectural Digest* she
was pretending to read, she picked up Marlena's *People*. She
couldn't look at anyone else's dream house with her own
falling apart.

CHAPTER 30

Frozen Phlegm

YELLOW GUNK. A charming side effect of the new medicine her doctor had put her on after her last checkup. An increase of phlegm. For half a second Laura felt like she'd blacked out, but she hadn't. She coughed it up and life resumed.

Laura and Ben were having dinner, sitting side by side in a booth at Dominic's. Their hips touched and Laura had her hand on Ben's thigh through most of dinner. He had caught her episode when it happened. He spoke to her in a low tone and said, "You're okay, just relax," which turned out to be the perfect thing to say.

They were eating Dom's famous fried potatoes, salad, and burgers. She stopped in mid-chew. It froze, her chewing muscle, on the potato-onion-garlic combo she'd been masticating. The Tasty Combo was stuck at the back of her throat. Like the conveyer belt had just stopped cold and it shocked the shit out of her. It was another first. Damn, she thought later that night, when she remembered the moment. For a second she thought she'd choke to death. A split nanosecond, and then she'd snapped to and remembered what her doctor warned her about the new drug. She'd also read about it in the "what to expect" column on Michael J. Fox's website. He was the best thing that ever happened to

Parkinson's Disease, Laura thought, when she'd first gone on his website.

Talk about taking on the sins of the world. Michael J. Fox was so young and so atypical for the disease, and he'd been its angel. *Nothing is an accident, and it's all about how to use it. For good. Or shit.*

She also thought how much better life was with Ben.

Who would she leave him for? The handsome dude in the waiting room waving his arms to beat the band? There was no one, and she knew it. Her anger at those things would never change it, just exacerbated her symptoms, and exhausted her. It was that anger that had been choking her all along. Her therapist practically yelled it at her the other day during their session. Guess she was finally fed up with them, not hearing it in her normal tone over the last two years.

"You two are never going to get it," said Monica, the therapist. "Whatever you didn't get then, it's *over, stop looking,* you aren't going to get it."

Over. Stop thinking, expecting, being disappointed. You're not getting it.

You didn't get the love you needed from your mother, Ben. You didn't get the love you needed from your father, Laura. So move on.

"She's not your mother," Monica told Ben, speaking of Laura. "She'll go away and come back." Laura, who, when she went away, had no intention of coming back, ever. But after a day hiding out in her friend Molly's guest house. She always did.

When the choking stopped at dinner, Laura remembered to take smaller bites and chew her food well. *If a freeze should occur somewhere in the throat or if the phlegm gets stuck . . . food and phlegm, now there's a disgusting duo . . . breathe through the nose and relax the throat and the food can just slip right on down, smooth sailing.*

That made perfect sense, Laura thought, even if much of the time not much else did. Before falling asleep that night she moved her body into the "position," a thing she hadn't done in weeks. Inched it across the bed to Ben and slid tush first into his stomach. Glued together by warm flesh, primally connected, they fell asleep happy to be home.

CHAPTER 31

Remorse

REMORSE. IT CLUNG to her. It sunk into her pores like the cream she moisturized with daily. A thin film that she constantly reapplied, layered on again and again. She didn't think of remorse the way she thought of anger, sorrow, or disdain. She didn't have to. It had become a part of her, a second skin that, knowing it was there, she had forgotten about.

Until she remembered.

Laura wasn't sleeping well those days. She slept a lot, but not well.

There was too much going on in her mind to let her sleep the sleep she longed for. The sleep that would allow her to wake up feeling refreshed, energized, and renewed. That's the sleep Laura longed for. The sleep she got was filled with scenes from her life. Scenes of remorse.

There was so much of it, sometimes she wondered how she'd made it that far.

Walking with Gracie the other day, they'd talked like best friends. Mother and daughter, yes, but also best friends who knew each other so well certain things didn't need to be said.

Walking along the beach, their feet in sync, splashing through the water, chilling their toes, sending shivers up their calves, Laura sensed her mother walking beside them. The ocean was her mother's favorite place. Her mother's happy place. Again, there was remorse. Sorrow that she had never walked along the beach with her mother talking truth. Even though it wasn't her responsibility at thirteen, it wasn't her job to initiate the conversation, Laura still felt remorse. She knew. She had always known. There were many times she and her mother had stood side by side, feet planted in the sand, baby waves breaking and rolling over their ankles, that she could have said something.

"Mommy, what is really going on with you?" could have been the opening line. "I know there's more than you're telling us," could have followed it.

So many late afternoons that summer, the summer before she died, she'd spent with her mother either in the pool or the ocean when everyone else had gone home.

Between five P.M. and six P.M., the lifeguards left, the beach boys brought all the green chairs and striped umbrellas back up to the "beach boy shack," the snack bar closed, and peace descended.

That was her mother's time. The pool was empty. No one yelling "Marco Polo." No thirteen-year-old girls in madras bikinis practicing their diving skills for the lifeguards. Laura would hold her mother by the elbow and walk her into the shallow end where she would let her go. Her mother relaxed, a smile that said "I'm in heaven" spread across her face, as her legs fanned out beneath her. Laura could see her mother in the powder-blue bathing suit she wore that summer, see her cleavage as she floated uninhibited from one side of the shallow end to the other.

There was so much they could have said, but Laura remembered little of what they did say. After the pool, she would walk her mother down to the ocean. A short journey that at times felt like a thousand miles. Her mother couldn't use her walker in the sand, so Laura was her walker.

Picking one foot up almost to her knee, then the other, with Laura steadying her as she walked, they made it to the shore in excruciatingly slow time.

When they got there, again her mother rewarded her with that smile. The smile that made them both forget the getting there. Feet in the ocean, she came alive.

What did they talk about though? Laura wished she could remember even the most mundane sentence that passed between them.

After their own beach walk, Grace told Laura she felt better now that she knew what was going on. She assured Laura that she knew what she wanted. Assured her that she'd be with her mother on every step of her journey.

Exhaling, Laura felt relieved. Gracie was the only one who could walk her down to the ocean. Maybe if she'd been twenty-six instead of thirteen, her mother would've talked to her. Said things she would have remembered.

Laura could picture her mother's red polished toes in the water and felt the remorse catch somewhere in the back of her throat.

She was doing things differently. Small comfort that it was.

CHAPTER 32

Slithering Lizard

SHE HAD HAD a bad dream. She'd been thinking about it all day. She needed to go back and dissect it several times to see what the message was. She thought there was more than one. One was about her death. That was more of a physical feeling than thought though.

Laura was sitting in her doctor's office two days earlier, sitting minding her own beeswax, as they used to say, flipping through a *People*, always a comfort food, noting how absolutely weird Kim Kardashian's big fat ass was in that tight white skirt, and how could anyone in their right mind feel attractive in that skirt with that ass, when the handsome white-haired guy across from her reading *Golf Digest* started flailing.

Fucking flailing. Arms up in the air at right angles sort of, going back and forth, right to left, on their own volition. She had seen it before, but that time it scared her. Lost in the ugliness of Kimmy K's ass, she nearly made a sound but flinched instead. It took her a couple of seconds to understand what was happening to the guy across the way who had a youthful face under that nice, still thick, head of white hair. Her heart broke for him. She hadn't let that in before. Had steeled herself against what would inevitably be her. Holding in the urge to cry so hard her chest throbbed with pain. Then her pulse accelerated so fast that that scared her too.

She hurt so much she wanted so badly to let it all go. She couldn't do it to the poor guy though. He'd think it was his fault and feel even worse than he did already, she thought. She'd start shaking, his flailing would accelerate, and they'd have a helluva Jamaican dance party going on.

Sitting in her doctor's office after her examination, her doctor explained the flailing. Said it's not uncommon. An uncontrollable impulse with Parkinson's Disease. Oh, and the depression she was feeling, that was part of the disease too.

No, ya think, Doc?

Turns out it was something having to do with the dopamine creating imbalance in the serotonin levels. *Blatty blah blah blah.*

"OK," she'd said to the good doctor, "so whadda we do? Gimme more pills, or do I smoke more dope?"

"Hmmm . . . that's another consideration. Too much pot smoking can cause depression too."

"OK," Laura said again, "Parkinson's causes depression, pot causes depression. I'd rather cut down on the Parkinson's." The good doctor laughed.

Laura liked having her doctors think she was funny. Needed them to like her. If they liked her, they'd take better care of her. Or so her thinking went. Although her mother's doctor, Dr. Styner, loved her mom and she still died.

She thought the flailing incident influenced the other part of her dream the previous night. So many things were going on at once. She was back in high school and there was a graduation ceremony going on. Her uncles and some of her cousins were there and she felt nauseous and was crawling. She couldn't get up. She had no strength and dragged herself, crawling like a dying lizard, around the campus. Dark green, scaly, and shiny, she could barely inch her lizard body across the fresh-cut grass to the podium. Shedding scales in the grass as she laboriously tried to crawl, she realized she was getting nowhere.

In the dream, she wished she could've been a dying mermaid instead of a lizard. She'd rather cut down on dreaming than pot.

CHAPTER 33

Playing Outside the Box

SHE HAD REACHED the age of wisdom. Here's the wisdom: you can't depend on anyone for happiness. You make your own. Armed with that knowledge, she decided to have that affair. The one she fantasized about in the bathroom with Grace when she looked in the mirror and scared the shit out of herself. Knowing what she knew, and given the state of her health, it was the best possible choice. And the least possible.

With her tremors lessening from the new med she was on, the one that made her choke up Dom's fried potatoes, she decided to get on with it and stop wasting time. She had no more to waste.

Really, though, who would want a lover whose head bopped like a dashboard doll? Or whose feet froze in place just as she was moving in for an embrace. Very few people, that's who. Unless they had aberrant fetishes. She didn't want a lover with aberrant fetishes, she just wanted someone hot and funny. Hot, willing, and funny. That wasn't much to ask. No brains, bank account, or bravery needed.

That was her takeaway from their last family trip; it was time to go outside of the family unit. Her child, on her own path clearly creating her own life, Ben, well, Ben was just becoming old. Old Ben. Old Ben was the same as young Ben except a little deafer and a little more afraid.

Laura put white light around herself when Ben went into fear. She couldn't allow any of his fear to seep into her pores and become a part of her. No, she was constantly on guard when it came to Ben and his anxieties. For years she took them on, wrongly thinking she could help him, calm him, alleviate or shorten the list a bit. But she knew that it was never part of her job. She knew, too, that the window of opportunity for an affair could close any minute so she'd better put a move on.

It had been so long. She had never cheated on Ben. For years she'd been the model par excellence of the faithful wife. At first, she thought she wouldn't know how to go about it. One couldn't walk into a market, a department store, a restaurant, yelling, "Hello, I'm looking for a lover—someone hot and hysterically funny and not afraid of a decaying woman. Anyone here fit the bill?"

Yet it was an idea firmly rooted in the forefront of her mind that, once rooted, would happen. That's how things had always worked for her.

Sometimes she thought if her mother had had a lover, maybe she would have lived longer. Maybe she would not have been in such a hurry to leave her three young girls and drunken husband. Maybe? But for a devout Catholic, that wasn't an option. Can't be a martyr if you leave the liquored-up louse.

Laura made a mental note to check "devout" in the dictionary. Perhaps it was time to become a devout hedonist. Make hay while the sun was shining. Or the head wasn't shaking off the neck. Be naughty or be dead. Given the choice, she'd go for naughty any day.

Hmmm . . . new underwear. That was a start. Buy lingerie and he will come!

At least I haven't shaken off the ability to amuse myself. New underwear? Really? Could it be as simple as that?

CHAPTER 34

Not Denzel

HE WASN'T BLACK the way she had so wanted him to be. That was Denzel's fault. Good cop, bad cop, whatever he played, Denzel had been her heartthrob for years. The guy was the anti-Denzel.

He was white, gray-haired, with a totally average body. He was also smart, made her laugh, and had bad-boy eyes. She'd never want to be with him forever; she loved going home to Ben. A totally perfect affair.

He lived near Butterfly Beach, where they both walked their dogs. Her short and sassy Wayne developed a boy crush on his formidable shepherd, Luke. Eventually they started walking together. Walking led to coffee at Pierre Lafond and God knows where coffee might lead to again. Laura was still justifying her actions at that point, but the main thing was that he took her out of the sameness, the anxiety, and the pain of what was happening to her . . . to them, to her and Ben.

An affair might not be the answer. She knew that and might be ending it soon, perfect as she thought it was. She hadn't counted on the nagging sense of guilt. It left her much more energetic than she'd been in years though. She was learning so much about jazz. The anti-Denzel taught American Contemporary Jazz at the University of California,

Santa Barbara. He'd spent years playing with heavyweight jazz bands. He became fascinated with the theory that jazz pianists and classical pianists have different brain activity. "I can almost hear that bebop mind of yours heading straight to Chick Corea," he said one afternoon. "Bebop!" she replied, pretending to be insulted. "Okay, hummingbird-mind. Better—Lady." Quite clever, her Piano Man, and very sexy. He still had the naughtiness in his eyes Ben used to have.

She missed Ben's naughty eyes. She missed Ben, and that guy, good as he was, wasn't Ben. But neither was the real Ben, and that was the rub. Right there. The thing about Ben, which had been the thing about him from the beginning, was that she trusted his heart. He was the most pure-hearted man she'd ever met. The other stuff, the "frugality," aka penny pinching, the need for control, and his anxiety, which he'd swear under oath he didn't have, were merely old installations.

But . . . hello . . . look at me, she thought. What the hell had I lost in my eyes, my body, my mind, and heart? She began to think her little affair wasn't because Ben was gone. It was because she was gone. That's what she really wanted back. Herself. Herself before she went from painter to Mother of the Year to invalid. Before she became a shaky bag of bones breaking dishes and unable to open jelly jars. Before Ben's morning greeting changed from "Good morning, my love" to "How do you feel today?" A question she hated because it reminded her that she'd gone. That the woman who stood before him was just a fragile fraud. It was a question the Piano Man never asked.

CHAPTER 35

Not a Mercy Fuck

HER LEG FROZE on top of his. They had fallen asleep like that, her left leg hooked over his, after making love. She lay awake for at least five minutes, trying to move it so she could get up and go to the bathroom, but it wouldn't budge. She even tried humming to get it going, as ridiculous as she found that bit of advice when she first read it on the PD website. Oh, yeah, when limbs freeze, try humming or singing as that sometimes triggered the brain to get them going. Yeah, I'll be doing that, Laura had thought to herself. I'll break into "How Much is That Doggie in the Window" when I'm stuck in bed with the Piano Man.

Desperate to get up, get dressed, and get home, though, she sucked it up and hummed. Nothing. Hummed a different tune. Still nothing. Sang a few bars of "Happy Birthday," which, under pressure, was the only song she could think of after the "How Much is That Doggie" song, and still, nothing. Instant karma, she thought. Payback for being an adulterer. Paralyzed for life.

"Hey, you, whose birthday is it?" said anti-Denzel, waking beside her.

"Hmmm no one's; I'm just fooling around."

"Oh, trying to be subtle, huh . . . is this you saying you want to fool around some more? A little Marilyn/JFK croon into my ear? It's cute. I like it."

Flushing from the base of her neck, Laura felt trapped and stupid. Feeling the hot pink moving up toward her cheeks, she went silent. Knowing that stressing over how to explain it would make her leg stay frozen longer, she closed her eyes, pretending to rest a bit longer. Silent. They both lay silent a little longer. His house was set back from the road and so quiet. No house noise, no street noise. Lying there she heard the birds outside. Black birds squawking from the trees behind the house. Getting ready for their late afternoon flight over to the Biltmore to forage food.

She needed to get up and get home. Ben had driven down to LA for a meeting and would be back for dinner. She wanted to shower and change and free her body and mind of that bedroom before he got home.

Humming, singing, and what was the other ridiculous thing she read that might send the move message to her limbs?

"What's wrong?" he asked softly. She said nothing at first and as she was about to audibly say nothing again, he asked, still softly only stronger and fuller, "Is it MS?"

Shocked, she said, "No, it isn't MS."

"Then what is it, Parkinson's?" He said that in such a matter-of-fact way. No longer shocked, she felt completely exposed. If she could jump up and run out of the room, away from that bed, she would. But she couldn't. Instead she just lay there tasting the saltwater streaming down her cheeks.

"It's all right, darlin', I've known for a while, although I was thinking it was MS."

The way he called her *darlin'* with such natural affection, as if he'd called her that a thousand times before, almost took the sting out of the rest of what he'd said. He'd known. She didn't think he knew. Didn't want him to know. Needed him not to know.

Gushing like a broken faucet, she wiped her face with the sheet. Fuck it, she thought. If he can call me *darlin'*, I'm using his sheet like an overgrown hankie. There was nothing else she could do but lie there and cry. The jig was up. He could see her with all her secrets exposed like the loosening flesh on her upper arms.

Softly she began to hum the lullaby she used to sing to Grace when she was a baby, a combination she made up of "Hush Little Baby" and "My Girl." "Hush, little baby, don't say a word," she hummed, then sang in her lowest and littlest voice and then, like magic, she moved her leg.

Grabbing his shirt which had ended up on her side of the bed, she held it up to her chest, slid out of the bed, and walked to the bathroom. She dressed and washed her face. She drank a cup of water from his toothbrush cup, then washed her face again. She needed to go home. She knew he had given her something just then, but he'd also taken something away. Something she needed and wanted and thought she had found in him. Even if just for a little while. And then it was gone.

And that was heartbreaking. The last thing she wanted out of that, whatever it was they had, was a mercy fuck.

CHAPTER 36

Really, Miss L

LAURA HAD GONE to sleep thinking about Matthew, aka her Piano Man. Since the shift had occurred, she called him by his given name, Matthew. The shift, of course, occurred the day she walked into his house unannounced after not having seen or spoken to him for three weeks. Three weeks and five days to be exact.

When he said he knew just how damaged she was, she shook her way to the front door. She hadn't planned on marching herself back in like that, but she did, and to her relief and heart's delight she was welcomed back with open arms. What that was she couldn't label. As much as she'd have liked to for comfort's sake. She had always needed to label, to categorize and have a handle on whatever the situation was. Even way back when her daughter was in grade school, "Mean Girl," "puberty," "adolescent behavior," and way back before that, "drunk" and "no good son of a bitch." All labels she knew, understood, and used. Even with Ben, "work crisis," "midlife crisis," "TV producer crisis"—they all had a label.

That. That what? Friendship? (*Affair* was a word she hated.) Yet it had no label, and as such, had no limits. Scary with a capital *S*.

"So be scared," Matthew said the other day. "Allow yourself to be scared. Then ask yourself what your fright is really about." Is he a musician or a frigging therapist? was her immediate thought.

"Easy for you to say," is what she said.

"Really, Miss L?" The way he said it was both playful and endearing. And sweet. She liked that he'd given her a nickname.

"Really? You think this is easy for me? That I have nothing to risk, letting you into my heart? Allowing myself to open up to the glory of Miss L." That last line he said with a smile, moving in to nuzzle her neck.

They were in his bedroom, lying on his bed fully dressed. The french doors leading to his backyard were wide open. They'd been lying on the bed talking, feeling the breeze blow in from the beach a few blocks away. Laura was admiring his yard. Having noticed his rose garden off to the right needed some TLC, she'd asked him if he knew about saving his coffee grounds and eggshells, how they were wonder foods for roses.

Easy. What they had was easy. One moment she could talk to him like he was a friend she'd known for years, sharing her gardening tips, and the next moment they could segue into kissing and holding each other like teenagers, giddy with each other's scent.

His bedroom was uncluttered. Simple and spare. The bed, an oak dresser that looked to be older than both of them combined. A brown leather reading chair with a Navajo blanket resting over its back. No sleek flat screen. A small expensive speaker on his nightstand, and a portal for his iPhone so he had his music. A stack of books on the floor. No art. Just the french doors opening to nature's art.

All that seemed to matter was that she was herself in that room. Herself in a way she hadn't been for years. It was safe and real, and more than ever, she needed to be who she was in that room, a woman who wore sexy underwear and didn't tell her dead mother she'd be joining her soon.

CHAPTER 37

Found Money

"WE ARE ALL in mourning. All of us. Some of us don't even know who or what we are mourning, but trust me, we are all in mourning."

He said that lying in bed with one arm around Laura's naked shoulder. They were in his bed that had become her sanctuary. Having abandoned the thought of giving him up, she had allowed herself to sink into whatever was going on there. Allowed herself to sink into him. Just as she allowed her body to sink into his touch, she'd allowed her heart to melt into whoever he was and whatever he was open to giving her of himself.

Laura'd gone from thinking it was wrong, to feeling it was a gift from God. Whatever went on between them had nothing to do with Ben, or Grace, or the life she'd created with them. It was there. It was intact. She was still giving at that office. Her Piano Man, though, was just for her. It was like the hundred-dollar bill she found in an old jacket. A surprise. A gift. Found money to spend as she wished. And nobody's business but hers.

The last time they were together, Laura took a long time in his bathroom, getting dressed. His bathroom, a bachelor's for sure, simple, no fuss no muss. He still used Old Spice, the white ceramic bottle being the only décor except for a photograph of a sailboat he'd once owned. She had a flash-back of that kind barkeep, Rudy, and the beautiful boat he gifted her with. She hadn't a clue what happened to that boat. It must have sailed away like so many things in her life.

Laura took a long time getting dressed because her leg was frozen, and her right hand shook so much she had a hard time getting her jeans on. When she finally came out, he said nothing. She mumbled something about being late, avoided looking him in the eyes, and left.

That night she told Ben she felt she was fighting some-thing and slunk into bed. They ate dinner on trays and watched a movie.

When she got up to go to the bathroom in the middle of the night, Sammy Davis was on her wall. He wasn't dancing or singing, just smiling. On her wall larger than he was in life, which would have pleased him.

"Ben, wake up, Sammy Davis is on the wall."

"Is he tap dancing?"

"No, he's just smiling, get up, you've got to see him."

"Oh, shit, I see Dean and Frank there with him. Dean's got a drink in his hand," said Ben, sitting up.

We both knew what was happening. The hallucinations. One of the finer perks of PD. Instead of getting scared or sad or shaken up, they both burst out laughing. Every time one of them started to calm down, the other said something silly making fun of the whole thing until they were rolling off the bed.

It was good. It was us, Laura thought, Me and Ben.

∽

WHEN SHE arrived at Matthew's house a few days later, he greeted her with peonies in hand. He took her straight into his bedroom, where he had arranged a tray of tea and cookies—like she was his visiting grandmother, not his lover.

"And this is because?" she said, looking at him with one eyebrow cocked.

"This is because we are going to get under the covers and get cozy. We are going to get warm and drink tea and eat cookies, and you are going to tell me how long you've had Parkinson's. And then I am going to kiss you where you tell me it hurts."

With that Laura started to cry. Not loudly or uncontrollably. Not even audibly. Silently with fat wet ovals rolling down her cheeks.

"Come on now. You're safe here. We're both safe here. I've made it that way."

He had. After his wife died, seven years earlier, he redid the house they bought together and lived in for almost thirty years. He'd stripped it down instead of making it into a shrine of memories of her, of them, and the life they had. If anything, it was an ode to simplicity. A respite from the done and overdone. Having been stripped, it begged one to leave all excess at the door.

"I'm not here to save you," he said. "I'm just here to spend time with you. To enjoy you. There's nothing I want from you other than what we give each other."

So simple, Laura thought. So simple it was almost too simple to bear or to believe.

"A while. I've had it for a while," is all she said when she could talk. She said it flatly.

"Ah," said the Piano Man . . . silence. The silence stretched, and Laura felt her heart start to race.

But he broke the silence with a short laugh. "Ah, well, that means I get to kiss you from the top of your head all the way down to your toes," he said, taking her teacup and placing it on his nightstand. "You ready, girl?" He asked that in the gentlest sexiest voice she may have ever heard.

Later, lying there, hands touching like teenagers, they talked. "We are all mourning our losses . . . love, youth, innocence, health . . . so we must snatch joy wherever we find it."

Yes, she thought, as she burrowed further down into their cotton-sheeted nest. *That's what this is between us . . . it's my joy.*

CHAPTER 38

This Little Piggy

SHE THOUGHT ABOUT the chocolate-covered cherries again that morning. She hadn't thought about that incident in a long while. It was like a recurring nightmare, but instead it was something real that happened when Laura was a little girl. It had been more than fifty years and still it came to visit. Always without warning or invitation.

Lying in her own bed, Laura was stretching and tightening her feet, getting them ready to hit the floor and start a new day when the memory slid right in. She'd gotten to tightening and releasing her right calf, then—boom, bang— she was back with the chocolate-covered cherries in the silver-and-red foil wrapper.

She was seven. They were living in the old house. It was an ordinary night, except her father had brought home a box of chocolates. When he walked in the front door, he had his hat in one hand and a silver-wrapped package the size of a shoebox in the other. Laura and her sisters were concerned with the contents of the box. The shiny silver paper intrigued them to distraction. Her father had brought home the delicious chocolate-covered cherries for an after-dinner treat. A rare occasion.

When dinner was finished, he got up from the dining room table and went into the kitchen and came back with five silver-and-red-wrapped domes, one for each of them, including her mother and himself. Laura had hers unwrapped and sitting in the palm of her hand before anyone else. It was to her a thing of true beauty. The milk chocolate dome felt warm, solid in her hand. She bit into the top and saw the cherry floating in thick pink liquid and quickly put it to her lips before any of the liquid spilled out. The cherry juice combined with the smooth chocolate shell felt like Christmas morning in her mouth! Laura sucked the liquid out of the chocolate dome while her tongue played with the cherry until she couldn't stand it any longer and ate the whole candy.

It was the most delicious thing she had ever tasted. She immediately wanted another. She thought of the box her father had walked in with; there had to be many more chocolates in that box.

"Can I have another one, please?" she asked, chocolate on the corners of her mouth.

"How about saying 'Thank you' instead of being a pig and asking for more," replied her father, causing her cheeks to redden like the cherry inside of the chocolate.

After his answer, neither one of her sisters asked for more but in unison said, "Thanks so much, Daddy," like the good girls they were. Not the pig Laura felt like at that moment.

Later that night, walking past her parents' bedroom on her way to the room she shared with Lucy, something shiny and silver on top of her father's dresser caught her eye. The overhead light was on, illuminating the dresser top. Her parents were downstairs watching the news on TV. Laura went into the room. Her immediate hope was that it might be another chocolate-covered cherry and she couldn't resist going in for a closer look. It was a stack of new silver coins, dimes, and quarters, and without thinking Laura picked up one of the dimes, holding it between her thumb and index finger for inspection.

"What are you doing?" her father's voice demanded from the doorway. So lost in the shiny treasure, Laura hadn't heard him come up the stairs and had no idea how long he'd been standing there.

"Put my money down," said her father, staggering toward her, the corners of his mouth twitching. The "tell" was on. The corners of his mouth twitched after three drinks. "Put my money down," he commanded again. "I give you chocolate, but it isn't enough, so you ask for more. And now, instead of being grateful, you're stealing my money."

Stealing money? The idea hadn't even crossed Laura's mind. Finding another chocolate-covered cherry, yes, that had crossed her mind, and if she'd found one, she knew in her heart that she would have wanted to take it. She had not thought about the dime, though, except for how shiny it was.

"You are a greedy little pig," slurred her father. "I give you a treat, you just want more."

Laura could feel the heat back in her cheeks. Feel them turning pink, the color of a pig. She stood there, aware of her short legs and her plump tummy and the pink cheeks and knew even though the corners of his mouth were twitching, that her father was right. She was a pig. That was the memory, the scene that revisited her many times over the last six decades. She never knew what unleashed it, although it wasn't from lack of thinking.

Later that afternoon, driving over to see Matthew, she sensed the little girl with the short legs, plump tummy, and pink pig cheeks sitting there in the passenger seat beside her.

CHAPTER 39

Up the Weed

SHE USED TO marvel at people who lived with pain daily. Physical pain, that is, as emotional pain she'd always understood to be one of life's givens. Maybe marvel wasn't the right word. Maybe it was fear dressed up as marvel. It was a door she hoped she'd never have to open. Maybe if that kind of pain came knocking, she'd just pretend she was deaf until it stopped knocking and went elsewhere. Not so. It knocked and knocked. It knocked until she finally had to say, shut the fuck up, I'm coming.

Laura always knew she had little to no tolerance for physical pain. When she was eight, she ran away from the doctor's office in her underpants just as he was preparing to give her a shot. She ran all the way down Central Avenue in her white cotton Carter's before her mother caught up to her in the family station wagon and dragged her back.

Years later when she was going through fertility problems that demanded weekly blood tests, she self-medicated with Valium beforehand. That had to stop when the nurse informed her that the Valium could affect the test results.

Her daughter, Grace, once had a tooth drilled, then filled without Novocain. Laura forgot the particulars of why but remembered how absolutely beyond impressed she was with her offspring's ability to withstand the pain.

It was her constant companion those days, pain. She'd have thought that the humiliation of the outward manifestations of Parkinson's was punishment enough. Walking through her old gallery with her head bopping to beat the band? Mortifying. The loss of her one true talent, her ability to paint. Out the window, as the expression went, due to a right hand that trembled at will. Having never been consulted by the powers-that-be as to just what was enough punishment, or karmic retribution, she was learning to live with that which she had always feared.

"But, Doc," she had said to her physician, whom she got a kick out of calling Doc, stiff gent that he was, "what's this pain in my right side all about?"

"Describe it," Doc replied.

"Like a thick blade that twists at will," Laura answered without pause, focusing on the red arrow in the Calder print in his office. The blade was twisting as she spoke, so zooming in on the print was a trick she hoped would help.

"I'm not actually sure," replied Doc, petting his tie. Hermès, with flying elephants. Petting the silk to help him think, perhaps.

"My guess is it's the medicine you're on now. One of the side effects we spoke about, remember, is how it affects your kidneys. It might be from the medicine. Or it could just be one of the internal effects of your disease. Do you want something for the pain? You could always smoke some more marijuana." A sure sign he was at a loss. Last year, it was "cut down on the weed."

"Sure Doc, I'll smoke more weed," she said, eyes on his high-priced flying elephants.

Up the weed, go visit my Piano Man. Deal as best we can. Isn't that what it had come down to? The Piano Man part she kept to herself.

CHAPTER 40

The Creative Whack Pack

SHE'D GONE FROM apathy to despair. Even her Whack Pack said so. The card she picked was of a skeleton with a tombstone behind it. So much for the Whack Pack. Grace gave her the deck telling her to use it as a tool when she felt stuck. No pun intended Grace was good like that. She had all kinds of tricks up her sleeve, cards, books, daily affirmations to help her if, God forbid, she succumbed to not knowing her way.

Laura missed the Piano Man. He'd texted her several times. Funny, short messages letting her know he was there, waiting. Waiting for what? Laura thought. To get further involved with a situation that was going downhill. She thought of herself as a situation. The last time they were together, he said he could handle anything but chemo again. His wife had stomach cancer that several rounds of chemo during a three-year period didn't cure. Instead it turned her face gray; every hair on her head disappeared taking her spirit with it.

Laura felt that if she was the best he could come up with in seven years, he was as damaged as she was.

But God, she missed him. She'd stopped seeing him again. It had been almost three weeks, and to stop the roller coaster of thoughts and emotions regarding him, she slept. And picked cards from the goddamn Whack Pack.

She went from thinking it was good and that they connected in an unspeakable, intangible way, to they had a gift that was just theirs to share, to he was on a death trip and not his own; he was a watcher. Some days she thought she was crazy, denying herself whatever fix was available to her, and then, just as she would start to text him back, black thoughts came in and froze her texting fingers.

Why widen the audience? Hand out free tickets to the show? She got into bed and slept instead. She watched an old movie, *House of Spirits*. In it, Meryl Streep played a woman who could foresee the future. When she dies, the woman comes back to visit her daughter, who is dying in prison, and tells her she must choose life. She tells her daughter, who's lying on the cement floor of the prison, beaten and barely breathing, that she has work to do and her children need her, so she must choose life over death.

"You must choose life," Meryl the Ghost said, her ghostly white robes billowing in the nonexistent wind. "You must choose life" looped around and around in Laura's mind for days. But who needed *me*? she said into the loop. Who needed to bear witness to what was coming?

No one. It was why she'd been sleeping so much. She hoped her mother would come to her in a dream and tell her how to proceed. Because she was stuck. And it wasn't just her goddamn legs anymore; it was her spirit. It was frozen. There seemed no point in going on, as it would only get worse. It was guaranteed to end badly . . . Soon her mind would start going along with her body, and who needed to witness any of it? The hallucinations were coming more regularly. The other night she had rolled over, opened her eyes, and had seen a circus clown on her wall. She'd never liked clowns. Dead celebrities were much preferred. A repeat visit from Sammy would have been welcome. Elvis. Heard he got around a bit. No one needed to be a part of it, the craziness that was coming. She wouldn't text her Piano Man that day.

Not that day. She'd sleep, perchance to dream, and see what card she picked the next day.

CHAPTER 41

Knowing Nothing

SHE WALKED BY his house. She hadn't set out to do that, but she did. He was out of town giving a seminar and no one was there. She took Wayne to the beach and without thinking walked up the road. She could see his house, silently closed. Even closed it gave her comfort. The house was so simple in its wood-shingled structure, so unpretentious in its faded green trim.

Laura felt both good and childish walking by.

Like a teenage girl calling the boy she has a crush on and hanging up when she hears his voice. Maybe the whole thing was adolescent. Maybe that's where the adrenal rush, the excitement came from. The aliveness. There. There she had it. Aliveness. That was what she sought. Laura was feeling such a lack of aliveness in her life that she grabbed at whatever resembled it.

Monday. Her Mondays were always hard. She tended to do too much on the weekends. Pushing herself beyond her limits for others. Had since Gracie was little. Weekends Ben liked to socialize, so she was usually giving or going to dinner parties or art openings. Gracie had soccer games and birthday parties and, if she had no plans, Laura became the entertainment committee.

By Monday morning she was exhausted. Spent. In need of rest and renewal. That Monday was no different. She lay in bed for more than an hour, trying to feel her feet. They were numb. Both, which was unusual, as it was usually just one. It scared her the way each new symptom, each new level of loss, each new degree of her disease scared her. Was it a one-off? was the question. Or was that the way it was going to be from then on?

All day she fought the urge to say, "I'm dying." Ben was home working and had questions that required her attention. Every time he walked into her office with a new question, all she wanted to say to him was, "I'm dying. I couldn't feel my feet this morning for over an hour and it felt like they were dead. Like this is what's happening: I'm shutting down part by part."

Saying that would be wrong and serve no purpose. It wouldn't bring her relief or comfort or assurance that it really wasn't true. And it would freak him the fuck out.

She was confused as to the nature of her thinking. Was it instinct and knowingness, or just wishful thinking?

She wanted the day to be different. She could feel her feet. She got up and took her dog to the beach and then, accidentally on purpose, walked by Matthew's house again. It gave her comfort to see it there. Like a church, a chapel she went to for prayer and contemplation.

Laura was cognizant of the fact that she knew nothing. For many years it was important that she had answers, knew things, and could make decisions. But she knew that what she knew was nothing. Somehow she had to find comfort in that. That, and walking by the simple wood house with the green trim.

CHAPTER 42

What Will They Say?

GRACIE WAS DEALING with death for the first time as an adult. Her friends' parents had started to die. College friends with whom she was close, had lived with, pulled all-nighters with, cried over heartbreaks with, were grappling with loss. The last week, it was her roommate from her sophomore year's father. A doctor from Chestnut Hill, Philadelphia. He'd dropped dead on the golf course. On the ninth hole. Just like his own father had. He was playing with his two golf buddies. One was a cardiologist. The cardiologist could do nothing but pronounce him dead.

Grace called the other night to talk to Laura. She called because she was sad. She needed to hear her mother's voice. She needed to be reassured that Laura was still alive. She had just come from the wake, where she'd stayed more than two hours to support her friend. It was a real wake. No New Age LA service that she might have attended once or twice before, but a traditional funeral home wake. Very Main Line Philly.

The call was good. Going well until Grace said there must have been 200 people who came through to pay their respects just in the time she was there. She said her friend's mother was amazing, the way she stood on the receiving line in a simple black dress and pearls, thanking each person for coming. As her daughter spoke, Laura experienced a pang, a pain in her intestines. A flip to be exact. Occasionally, more than occasionally, that thing happened to her that felt like a muscle spasm or a "flip under," as she thought of it. It stayed there, flipping then hardening for a few seconds, causing excruciating pain.

By the time Gracie got to the part about how her friend's father was one of the best-loved professors at Penn medical school, which was after the part about the mother belonging to the Philadelphia Runners Club, Laura was bent, mouth wide open, silently gasping for air.

The flipped muscle wouldn't unknot.

Why, she thought, later that night, after she'd smoked half a joint to relax her stomach and coax the spasm out of the upper corner of her esophagus, was she such a narcissist. Why couldn't she just let the man die and have a million people go through his wake and another million take off work to go to his funeral without thinking about what would happen when she died? Why, she asked herself, was she so obsessed with who would attend her funeral? Or better yet, what would be said about her? Would anyone there march up to the pulpit, Kleenex in hand, to say good things?

What had she done that someone could talk about? Nothing. Nothing extraordinary. Nothing even of note. She felt the familiar panic. Was there time? Did she have time to save the pagan babies in Africa, or build housing for the homeless in Santa Barbara? Would they let her rock the orphaned babies at the hospital with her shaking hands? What could she do, and how much time did she have left to do it, so that when she died her family would be proud that she was theirs? That her daughter would be comforted by the fact that she was indeed a worthwhile person.

It was too deep, that sense of unworthiness she carried. She felt too tired to do something, anything that might compensate for that unworthiness.

Her heart beat rapidly, and her underarms were damp. Quickly. She needed to do something quickly, something brave. It didn't have to be so brave, but good. She needed to do something very, very good. Very good, then die while it was fresh, and someone could get up at the pulpit and talk about how good she had been.

Not for her, but for her Gracie. Maybe for her mother as well.

CHAPTER 43

Nice Tomatoes

LAURA PICTURED HER mother just the way she was back when she was alive, which she hadn't been in more than fifty years. That was perhaps not such a good sign. At that juncture in her life, Laura shouldn't have been keeping such constant company with her deceased mother. But she did. She thought about and talked to her regularly those days. Sometimes she felt her mother's spirit right there beside her. Looking down at her dog lying at the foot of her bed, stretched out yet on guard, ready to leap at any intruder, she saw Bosco, her mother's mutt. A hunter mix for sure, his tan body taut and his ears oval flaps, he fit the word hound to a T, old Bosco did. He was her mother's constant companion. She and her sisters, even her father, loved him and delighted in his escapades. Bosco prided himself on being on a first-name basis with every garbage man in Sands Point. Same with the mailman, and the milkman. He was loved by all, nice to everyone, friendly as a fool, but Bosco had only one love, Laura's mother.

When she was well, in the winter, Laura's mother spent her days in the living room, in her blue chair, a book on her lap and Bosco by her feet. She'd move outside to a lawn chair in the backyard during spring, summer, and early fall until the leaves had nearly fallen and the weather turned cold. Then it would be back to the blue chair again. Always, with Bosco lying at her feet. He went where she went. If she drove the car without one of us, he got the front seat. If she went out without him, he waited by the door for her to return.

Laura remembered him when she was young, during the good years. Her parents took a cruise to Bermuda every fall for a week, leaving their girls in the care of Hester, their boozed-up cleaning lady, and Bosco the dog.

He mooned around the house all day while the girls were in school, and lost weight because he wouldn't eat. Every night he slept in the girls' bedroom, watching over them. He was on the job. Hester, on the other hand, stayed drunk. Her parents' weeklong cruise flew by. Laura and her sisters felt well taken care of by Bosco. They mutually decided not to rat on Hester because they loved the Cott orange soda she let them have with dinner every night.

The previous summer, Laura had planted her first tomatoes. When the first one appeared, along with it came that smell, that overpowering, sweet, and distinctly new tomato scent. It was heavenly and unique unto itself. Laura inhaled deeply and was transported to her mother's backyard garden. It ran along the side of the garage at the end of the yard. There was a vine-covered grape arbor with tomatoes growing up outside of the garage wall. During the summer, her mom would be there late in the afternoons, wearing plaid Bermuda shorts with linen blouses, the sun starting to fade a bit behind her, her martini on the ground beside her while she picked tomatoes for the dinner salad.

It didn't take much—a whiff of a new tomato, the dog by her side—and there was her mother, birdlike legs sticking out of the Bermudas, reaching for her martini.

CHAPTER 44

The Bubble Wrap Situation

"W̲HAT'S GOING To happen when you can't walk anymore, Mom?" Grace asked. Twenty-seven and a business-
minded gal working for a well-funded urban planning firm,
she was all about proactivity and practicality.

I'll shoot myself.

"I'll cross that bridge when I come to it," she said.

"Yeah, well, how are you going to cross it, Ma, is the
question."

"Very smart-ass, don't you think, miss?" was Laura's
retort. "What do you want me to say, honey? In a wheelchair? If that's what I have to do, I'll do it."

Second lie of the day.

"Mom, I'm sorry. I don't mean to pressure you, but don't
you think being prepared will make you feel better? More
secure?"

"Oh, honey bun, I gave up that concept a while ago.
Being secure had to go out the window. It really did. Now I
find it's easier to just wake up, try to be grateful for the day,
do my best to live it, and be happy when I wake up the next
day."

"Mom, when you talk like that, you depress the shit out
of me."

I'm depressed myself. And it isn't helping to move the shit out of me, although that would be a perk. I'm numb and full of shit, constipation being another byproduct of PD.

That had been her reply to her doctor.

"How do you feel today, Laura?"

"Numb and full of shit."

Laura wanted to make Gracie feel better though. To stop worrying about her. She wanted them all to feel better and stop worrying about her, but she really wasn't sure how to do that.

Laura's mother had lied to her. To her and to her sisters. To that day, Laura didn't know if her father knew that his wife was dying or if she had lied to him too. For the last two years of her life, her mother had told them all she was getting better, that she was in treatment, having physical therapy, and recovering from the stroke that she said was the reason she couldn't walk, talk, or write legibly. Meanwhile she staggered, stumbled, and slurred so badly, onlookers would point. "Look, look at that woman—she's dead drunk!"

Recovering—while going from a walker to a *wheelchair?* Like they all were blind fools? Denial was good when it worked, but Laura knew she wasn't getting better, she was getting worse. What her mother couldn't tell her, the stabbing pains in her own stomach did.

Her own daughter made her promise that she wouldn't lie, but how could she tell Gracie the truth? That when she could no longer walk, she just wanted to get in the bed, close her eyes, and go to sleep. And not wake up the next morning. Not wake up to have someone help her dress and slide her into a chair. How could she tell her daughter that she wasn't that woman? That she wasn't brave? That she wasn't accepting, and that she really didn't love life enough to spend hers in a wheelchair wearing sopping Depends.

To make Gracie feel better, she'd say, yes, you're right. Yes, you're right, baby, I'm just having an off day.

An off day. She had run the scene in her head so many times. If she could still paint, she thought, maybe it wouldn't be so bad. She could do a small watercolor series instead of the large ones she always loved working on. Roll the chair up to the easel and work at that height or at a short table. If she could paint. But she couldn't paint. Not anymore. That ship had sailed several years before. The last time she tried to hold a brush, her hand shook so much that watercolors wound up everywhere except on the paper. Frustrated into angry tears, *she threw* all the paints and brushes to the floor.

So that idea was out. No painting from the chair.

And fuck it that she wasn't one of them, those many splendid souls who take their afflictions and run with them, wheelchairs and all. She saw them all the time. They sat in the waiting room at her doctor's office, in the waiting room of the lab where she got tested, in the hallway of the hospital when she got her MRIs, and what they were all doing—wearing those peaceful resigned smiles—was *waiting*. That's what they were doing. Waiting for more of their body parts to deteriorate until there was nothing left, and no place to go except into the ground. Or in a jar flung out to sea on a sunny day. No, that wasn't her. It never was and it wasn't going to be.

Grace was busy packing up the dishes Laura had given her for her new apartment. She'd given her a set of silverware and her blue and gold china. It felt effortless and good and in keeping with her aim to simplify and rearrange her life around the basics, as that's all she needed. Wedding silver and fine china and crystal wineglasses were never basics.

"Mom, if you allow yourself to think about it now and plan for it, when the time comes, you'll be ready to handle it." Her darling girl, smarter than smart, knower of so many things, needn't know that Laura had allowed herself to think about that, couldn't stop from thinking about it many, many times, and when the time came, she would indeed be ready.

"Don't worry, baby, I'll be ready. Right now, though, we've got a Bubble Wrap situation to handle."

CHAPTER 45

Cruising Through the Years

"HE TOLD ME I was fine." When Ben asked how her checkup went, she didn't have the energy to go into any more detail.

"Fine, he said you were fine?" Ben said. "Laura, this wasn't a pediatric appointment; you aren't ten. Come on, what did he say?"

"Ben, I'm tired. He didn't say anything new, I promise."

Laura was in fact exhausted from her checkup. It was a bimonthly ordeal or more, with blood tests, heart monitoring, arm waving, and a lot of bending and touching of toes or calves or whatever the hell she could reach in the lower leg region.

She knew Ben was being supportive. Just showing that he cared and was there for her. But she also knew something else. Her illness filled in something missing from his life. It allowed him to focus on her and her disease instead of himself and his production company, which was going south. For twenty years Ben's company turned out quality television dramas, making Ben, as one *Hollywood Reporter* writer dubbed him, "The Drama Maven of TV." Things had changed so much in the last five years, with "reality television" replacing drama series, that Ben was rethinking his future. He could only withstand that rethinking for so long.

Grateful to have somewhere else to direct his thoughts, he aimed them at Laura's failing health.

For years, all she wanted was for Ben to pay as much attention to her and her needs as he did to prime time slots. Since she had it, true to form, she really didn't want it. Nor did she need it.

"Did you take your pills this morning?" The question gave him a sense of purpose. To Laura, he sounded exactly like she did years ago asking twelve-year-old Grace if she'd taken her vitamins after breakfast. She felt like she was being smothered.

Ben's attention was also a constant reminder that there was something wrong with her.

"Honey, I take my pills, I do my exercises, I stick to my routine. Please can you just not ask me about it?"

"I'm just trying to be supportive," he said, looking like that scolded child again. "Isn't that what you've always wanted. Me to be more present, more supportive of you and what you're going through." His face had fallen; the scolded child was confused. Mommy, please, what have I done wrong?

Laura sensed that even if she explained it, he still wouldn't get it.

"Sorry, honey," she said, "I'm just tired. Am going to have a nap and then let's have a nice dinner and watch a movie." Even with his bottom lip in a pout he was as handsome as the day she met him.

Years earlier, she wouldn't have left the room until he made the happy face, but lately she wasn't buying in. Walking down the long hallway to their bedroom, her goal was no longer to put a smile on his face, but to lie on top of her white cotton duvet and sink into it. En route she surveyed all the family pictures that lined the hallway walls, a timeline of her life—Gracie as a baby, as a preschooler, the three of them sitting outside of their tent in the Serengeti, on the cruise ship in Greece, Grace's round six-year-old face so tiny beneath a wide-brimmed yellow rain hat in Maine . . . The pictures told the story of a good life. An incredibly good life. How the little girl on the bar stool at Rudy's grew up to have such a good life was both a mystery and a miracle.

She was grateful, but with sadness creeping through her veins, she was unable to show it. Crawling into her safe harbor, allowing her head to sink into the pillow, mentally lining up her gratitudes, she counted them one by one until she fell asleep.

CHAPTER 46

Shake Your Bad Self Lady

THE PULL TOWARD the other side had been too strong for too long. Laura had allowed it to go on. She saw that she'd been complicit in it. A willing victim, surfing those waters for almost two years, blinded by any other possibility.

Just recently she'd seen that there were indeed other options open to her. It demanded walking out of the comfort of the past though. Aha, there it was again, that word: *comfort.* There was comfort in her mother's story. Comfort in keeping it alive by becoming her mother. But Laura wasn't her mother and copycat crimes wouldn't bring her back.

PD. Parkinson's disease. Big Fucking Deal. Or not. Really, it was a choice. She remembered being at a holiday party where there was an attractive woman around her age at the buffet table, her head shaking to and fro in small demure shakes. The woman worked that buffet from one end to the other smiling, chatting, helping the man behind her by dishing out a scoop of whitefish salad onto his plate, head bopping the whole time. Not to mention that whitefish salad almost landing on the floor due to a trembling hand. "You shake your bad self," Laura wanted to say to her. "Go on, sister, bop your pretty self all over the room!"

Laura watched her as discreetly as she could. *A lot to be learned here, was her first thought. Choice. Wasn't it all in the choice?*

This dame has chosen to live, Laura thought. Simple as that. She could be the poster girl for PD, this pretty woman could. But me? I've been wallowing in an old story that isn't even mine. Disappointed with her husband, unable to cope with her marriage to a good-looking drunk, a good-looking nasty drunk, her mother allowed herself to go under.

"Only the good die young." Billy Joel was quoting an old Catholic riff there. One that Laura grew up with like it was the national anthem.

Her mother had died young, aka: good. "A tragedy." "Struck down in her prime." There were indeed different routes to take other than her mother's.

She used to love it when she was a little girl in a store or a restaurant with her mother and people would tell her she looked just like her mother. Later, as a young adult, whenever she ran into an old family friend who had known her mother and they said how much she resembled her, it made her day. For years, she scoured old photos of her mother searching for her own features.

It was a great love cut short. That's what it was. A primal bond, once broken, never had the chance to heal naturally. It was that break that had defined her life. But perhaps not her death. Laura had an epiphany. Dying wouldn't heal anything. It would only end something. She hadn't a clue, not a clue, how to do it differently. Although she sensed perhaps Matthew had been a start.

CHAPTER 47

Diana Sings Blue

LAURA DIDN'T SPEAK about Matthew, not even with her closest friend, Jan, her most evolved friend. Being so evolved, Jan told nobody anything, and on that level was the most trustworthy person Laura knew.

Keeping silent about Matthew wasn't easy. Laura had been tempted several times. Once or twice under the guise of figuring it out, once or twice seeking feedback. Specific feedback like "go for it" or "it's not hurting anyone," "you need it," etc., etc. But the truth was she felt too old to need permission and talking about him and what they had or what they did reduced both to levels they shouldn't be reduced to.

"Well, hello. You calling to say you are coming over or do you need me to beg? I will."

Laura laughed at the casual way he said it but was grateful that he made it so easy. The ease being part of the draw.

"Come in, we'll get into bed and then I'll make you an English muffin and we'll talk."

"Ah, you do know how to woo a gal, you tricky devil." Not long after she finished her retort, she was in his bedroom stepping out of her skirt and slipping under the covers. He was touching places she had forgotten even existed. Places in herself, in her body, feelings, dreams, that had been buried for years.

They never spoke about why she left. About why his knowing she was sick had sent her away. It was understood. And it was also understood that she came back. After making love, which was by turns both passion-filled and tender, they sat in his kitchen drinking tea and eating English muffins, listening to Diana Krall sing Joni Mitchell better than Joni ever did.

"Do you think she minds?"

"Does who mind what?"

"Joni. That Diana sings Blue so much better than she does."

"Well, Joni might not hear it as better. We're all so good at protecting ourselves by hearing only what we want to hear. But I'd imagine she'd feel flattered and relieved that someone is taking such beautiful care of her song."

"Hmm . . ." She took a bite of her English muffin. It was time to go home and make Ben dinner.

CHAPTER 48

Doing the Best We Can

*T*HERE IS TRUE *freedom in accepting loss.* Laura wished she'd known that years earlier, but the good news was she learned it before it was too late. She knew it the only true way one knew anything. From experience. *Loss is what we all try to avoid, although it is the unavoidable.* It was through loss that Laura found herself. Every time she'd lost someone, she had to go on. Since she was losing parts of her physical self, she was still going on. But it was different. It didn't define her anymore.

She wasn't the young teenager who lost her mother. She wasn't the older teen who lost her father. She wasn't the young woman who lost lovers. She was a woman, approaching old age, who, while losing her physical abilities, refused to let it define her.

Loss had been her go-to for so long though. Lately she had become obsessed with reading about the people living in camps having been forced from their homes in Syria, Afghanistan, and Iran. Doctors, lawyers, schoolteachers forced to give up their homes and herd their children like cattle through unknown pastures. Loss . . . what was the ability to hold a paintbrush compared to losing your home, your profession, your hopes and dreams for your children, and being forced to stand in line for hours to use the toilet?

What was losing one's ability to walk spryly down the street or hold one's head still compared to losing babies from malnutrition along the road to hoped-for freedom?

In thinking of that, that subject of loss, Laura gained comfort somehow in the choices she was making. Comfort in being able to accept what was given, however impermanent it might be. Comfort in grabbing joy where she found it. Comfort in letting go of the person she used to be.

Lying in Matthew's arms, she was cognizant of the peace she felt. It wasn't localized in her heart but permeated her entire being. Gone was any inner noise, judgmental chatter; the shoulds and shouldn'ts had vanished.

"It's fine. This is fine," Matthew had said.

"We can cherish each other and what we have and have no need to change it, make it more, make it different. Accept it and be grateful. When you are grateful there's no room for guilt."

"You are just the smartest guy!" Laura joked back to him, melting into his fingers as he stroked the top of her head.

"Life and losing. Life teaches you to lose gracefully if you let it."

"Who are you, Mr. Piano Man?" she asked, turning her head so he could stroke the other side. Wishing his fingers, his glorious fingers, would never stop. "I'm your consolation prize," he said, grinning, turning to kiss her.

She was so comfortable there in his room. In his house. It smelled of the ocean. She helped him tend his garden. Hand trembling, she pointed to the spot on the stem just above the cluster of five leaves where he should cut the roses. She had no desire to own him, his house, or his garden.

It's all just for now and always has been.

The mistake was thinking any of it was hers to hold on to. Hers for good.

It was all on loan.

Everything would go eventually.

That knowledge freed her. Freed her from her mother, her father, her vows to Ben. Freed her of anything and everything she still felt she owed to Grace. It was knowing that it was all going, everything she ever thought was hers, that freed her to love that man and not want to possess him. It allowed her to love her Ben and appreciate every inch of his heart.

And to understand that they were all doing the best they could.

Yes, there was freedom in loss. It allowed her to say, "Hold me please."

Epilogue

LAURA DIED WHEN she was ready.

And she died where she wanted to die.

Not in a hospital. She'd have none of that business. Home in her bed, the one she'd shared with Ben? Too weird.

She could never understand how people could do that, die in the bed where their spouse would continue sleeping.

The death bed. Weird and eerie and not her "jam," as Grace and her friends would say.

By the time her heart and soul told her it was time, Laura, who could've been a wonderful party planner in her prime, had the whole event mapped out.

She moved into a cottage at the El Encanto Hotel the week before. At her last appointment, her doctor, wearing his best Hermès tie, the one with bunnies, had told her it could be a couple of weeks "give or take." She went home, packed her white leather weekend bag with black piping, the one she bought for her first weekend away with Ben. The one she put on her first credit card, a Mastercard, and took almost a year to pay off. The one, all those years and leather bags later, was still her favorite.

The hotel had been renovated several years earlier. Unlike a lot of spruce-ups, it kept its traditional Spanish feel of warmth and subtle beauty. It was tucked into the Santa Barbara mountains, quietly and elegantly. It was a reminder of all that she loved about the area. The hotel also served a true English High Tea every afternoon that she loved. The diminutive sandwiches and scones slathered in clotting cream and jam were always her favorite treat.

The week she was there she ordered several tea setups from room service. She had no appetite, but it made her happy to see her nearest and dearest enjoying them. Both Lucy and Peggy had flown in to be with her and her best friend, Jan, had rented the cottage next door.

Even though being prone to slipping in and out of sleep, Laura got wind of the fact that Peggy was the one hoarding all the cucumber and cream cheese sandwiches.

"Didn't Mommy say she wanted to start having her New York friends over for tea when we first moved into Grandpa's apartment?"

Lucy said that from the overstuffed armchair next to Laura's bed and next to its twin occupied by Peggy. Grace sat at the foot of her mother's bed, bearing witness to the sisters' loving conversation.

"I can't believe I just remembered that."

"It's old age" Laura said, followed by, "What did you have for breakfast?"

"Haven't a clue," replied Lucy.

"There you have it," Laura said faintly. "I think I'll just close my eyes for a few minutes. I'm not going to sleep . . . just taking a little rest." She'd been holding Lucy's hand. "Aren't the cucumber sandwiches yummy?" barely made it out of her mouth before she drifted off.

Later that day a bouquet of roses arrived without a card.

"Oh," Laura said in what voice she had left, "from my Piano Man."

"I didn't know your mom took piano lessons," Peggy said to Grace.

"My father always said my mom liked to have one or two secrets up her sleeve. To keep her 'autonomy,' she told him. Playing Beethoven could have been one of them."

"I wouldn't put it past her," Peggy said, getting up to give Ben, who'd just walked in, her chair. Lucy got up on cue, letting go of Laura's hand. Ben then took Laura's hand in his two hands making her white and fragile fingers disappear.

"Oh, my honey's back," Laura said instantly, feeling his hands. "Peggy's been naughty and eaten all of the cucumber sandwiches. But tomorrow I'm saving them all for you. Lucy, don't take your eyes off her!"

Three days later she asked Ben to bring her a scone covered in cream and jam.

It took her almost a half an hour, but she finished the whole thing.

"That was perfect," she said. Smiling like, yet again, she might have a secret, she added, "Let's get in the position, Ben."

They did. She moved her tush into the spot against his stomach. When she heard his familiar sigh, quiet and drawn out, she closed her eyes.

Smooth. The way she wanted it. It was the smoothest event she'd ever planned.

What a good year for the roses
Many blooms still linger there . . .
The only thing I have to say
It's been a good year for the roses.

—ELVIS COSTELLO, "Good Year for the Roses"

Acknowledgments

THE FIRST WHOLEHEARTED thank you goes to my agent, Jim Stein, at Innovative Artists, for his amazing support and ability to read a hundred drafts of this book. The next, to constant, can-do, computer whiz Samantha Wheeler. And to publisher Judith Shepard, copy editor Barbara Anderson, and the rest of the staff at The Permanent Press.

To my husband, Jeff Stein, for his support and for being cool enough to not care if people think he's Ben.

To my mentors, Eve La Salle Caram and Kerry Madden, and to Alice McDermott, my teacher at Sewanee, who told me this was my novel.

Holly Palance and Helen Storey, my gold-medal trusted readers. And thank you to the Tuesday morning writing group for supporting Laura in her infancy.

A grand *merci beaucoup* to Lizières artists residency for gifting me with five weeks of serenity and silence in the French countryside so I could hear Laura's voice.

And to Francoise Kirkland and my daughters, Romy and Siena, for being my life support systems.

And, finally, to Mary Sheridan O'Neill for teaching me to be strong.

CPSIA information can be obtained
at www.ICGtesting.com
Printed in the USA
BVHW092241161022
648985BV00005B/9/J